D1281844

GOLDILOCKS WEDDING

Rayner wants her wedding to
be perfect, and asks her
friends to help. But April,
Lily have their own prob-
realises that even very
people need others
must deal with the
a break-in at her
is inundated with
unknown, and
factor. And as
find their
the surface
high, is her
really the
turning to?

Books by Carol MacLean
in the Linford Romance Library:

WILD FOR LOVE
RESCUE MY HEART
RETURN TO BARRADALE
THE JUBILEE LETTER
FROZEN HEART
JUNGLE FEVER
TO LOVE AGAIN
A TEMPORARY AFFAIR
FINDING HER PERFECT FAMILY
HER HIGHLAND LAIRD
SHADOWS AT BOWERLY HALL
HEART OF THE MOUNTAIN
A GERMAN SUMMER
MAID AT MUIRFIELD
PERFECT CHRISTMAS

SPECIAL MESSAGE TO READERS

THE ULVERSCROFT FOUNDATION
(Registered UK charity number 264873)

Established in 1972 to provide funds for
diagnosis and treatment of eye diseases.
Examples of major projects funded by
the Ulverscroft Foundation are:-

Children's Eye Unit at Moorfields Eye
London

croft Children's Eye Unit at Great
et Hospital for Sick Children
arch into eye diseases and
Department of Ophthalmology,
cester

Vision Research Group,
Health

heatres at the Western
London

almology at the Royal
Ophthalmologists

rk of the Foundation
leaving a legacy.
lly received. If you
e Foundation or
lease contact:

FOUNDATION
, Anstey
and

erscroft.com

CAROL MACLEAN

GOLDILOCKS WEDDING

Complete and Unabridged

LINFORD
Leicester

First published in Great Britain in 2019

First Linford Edition
published 2019

A catalogue record for this book is available
from the British Library.

ISBN 978–1–4448–4134–3

Published by
F. A. Thorpe (Publishing)
Anstey, Leicestershire

Set by Words & Graphics Ltd.
Anstey, Leicestershire
Printed and bound in Great Britain by
T. J. International Ltd., Padstow, Cornwall

This book is printed on acid-free paper

1

'You've heard of the Goldilocks Zone, haven't you? Well, I want my wedding to be like that.'

Goldie Rayner gazed at her three best friends in anticipation. A large diamond set in a slim old-gold ring glittered on her left hand. She took a sip of her skinny latte and sat on the edge of the coffee house sofa, her notebook perched on her knee with a chunky ink pen at the ready.

'Goldilocks?' They all chimed, and three gazes swung to Goldie's long brassy blonde curls.

She rolled her eyes. 'Surely one of you must know what I'm talking about?'

Lily sat opposite her on the other couch. She was wearing a faded purple velvet jacket over her favoured blue Indian cotton skirt. Goldie noticed a

1

crocheted flower brooch on one lapel and a cat hair on the other. That had to be from one of Lily's current strays. She pushed a strand of light brown hair behind her ears and wrinkled her freckled nose. Clearly, she hadn't a clue what Goldie was saying.

Beside her on the sofa, Rose sat staring into space. Rose was their resident dreamer, and Goldie wondered if she'd even heard a word of the conversation so far, apart from the Goldilocks question that had stunned them all. Then there was April. She sat in an upright wicker chair to Goldie's right-hand side. Although it was a Saturday morning in their usual cosy coffee hangout, she was wearing a grey business jacket and skirt, tights, and polished heeled shoes. Her dark hair was short and styled, but Goldie privately thought it too severe. April's gorgeous high cheekbones could've carried a gentler, longer cut.

Lily, Rose and April had been her best friends since she'd arrived in

England from America in the last year of high school. The other three had been besties since primary school years but had gladly opened their circle to include the exotic American. They had had more than a few wild escapades that year until the incident that sobered Goldie up and made her vow to settle down and study. Actually, it was more like The Incident, in capital letters, the way she thought of that horrible night. She brushed the memory away. She was here to chat about exciting things, namely her wedding to James. Besides, high school was ten years ago.

'Are you going to give us a clue?' Lily asked, nibbling on a gingerbread slice.

'It's got to be something to do with star gazing,' Rose said, stirring her cappuccino and making the chocolate dusting swirl into the cream. She smiled at her creation and stirred again.

'That's very perceptive of you, Rose.' April sounded quite surprised and slightly annoyed. 'I should have thought of that myself.'

Goldie hid a grin. It was inevitable in a group of four friends that some were closer than others. April and Rose were so different in personality that they occasionally rubbed each other up the wrong way. If she had to split them into twosomes, Rose and Lily were close, which left her with April. That had been the way it was at school. Sometimes she'd felt a bit left out when Lily and Rose were sharing a book or a joke. They'd be walking ahead while she was left to trail along with April. And April was hard to get to know. She didn't give much of herself out to anyone, even her best friends. She could be prickly and quick to take offence.

'You're not the only smart one,' Rose said. 'In fact, I think I have heard of the Goldilocks Zone. It's coming back to me now. It was on a television programme I watched. Isn't it to do with them finding new planets?'

'That's right,' Goldie said. 'It's how they decide if a planet is in the right zone to support life. It can do so if it's

4

not too hot and not too cold. If, in fact, it's just perfect. And perfect is what I want my wedding to be. Not too this and not too that, just right bang in the middle of the zone.'

'Trust you to think of your wedding in terms of astronomy,' Lily laughed. 'It's not just a hobby, it's an obsession.'

'It is not,' Goldie said. 'I like seeing the stars and reading about the heavens, that's all. I don't claim to understand all the maths and physics stuff or even the star charts.'

'Anyway, enough about planets,' April interrupted, glancing at her watch. 'I have to go soon, so can we get to the point, please?'

'Where do you have to go on a Saturday?' Rose asked. 'I was going to suggest we get another round of coffees and cakes. I'm quite happy to nestle in here for the next few hours. It's raining out there.'

'Yes, well, some of us have a business to run. Unlike your photography, which it appears can be done at any odd hour, my cakes are made to order and I've got an A-list actress who wants a party cake for tonight. My baker Sally's made the cake, but I need to get it decorated this afternoon.'

'Dressed like that?' Rose murmured.

April shot her a black look. Goldie hastily picked up her pen and flipped her notebook to a fresh blank page. She really didn't want April and Rose bickering. This was her moment, and they all needed to focus right in on the Rayner-Smith wedding.

'So the point is that I need your help to make my wedding perfect.'

'Shouldn't that be 'our wedding'?' Lily said mildly, brushing gingerbread crumbs off her long skirt. 'After all, my big brother is getting married too.'

Goldie blushed. 'Sorry, I meant our wedding. I get carried away by all the planning needed. James doesn't have to do anything except organise his stag night, rent a top hat and tails and turn up on the day.'

'He'll manage all that,' Lily said with

a grin. 'I suppose you're right, it falls to the bride and her mother to do all the work.'

'In my case, it falls to me only. Mom and Dad won't get here from the States until a week before the big day. You know what it's like with their jobs.'

Goldie's parents were both in the US military. As a child, Goldie hadn't spent more than a year at any one school in a variety of countries. Her year at Mayborough High had been the most stable time of her life up until then. When her parents had to leave to be stationed in Germany, Goldie had stayed on and boarded with a family until she went to the local college. She had desperately wanted to put down roots and have a normal life.

'How can we help?' Rose asked, leaning forward to listen.

'I thought it would be nice if you all contributed in some way. If . . . if you'd like to, that is?'

'Of course we will, you only have to ask.' Lily leapt up and came over and

7

hugged her tightly. 'I can't believe you're going to be my sister-in-law as well as one of my very best friends.'

Goldie felt her eyes moisten. She wanted to hug them all. They were her family. In fact, they were more family than her own parents whom she never saw. She'd emailed them to tell them she was getting married and it had taken a week for her mother to email back. She blamed the terrible internet connection in South Korea, but Goldie had her doubts. Still, at least they had promised to come to the wedding.

'So . . . ' She squeezed Lily's hand. 'I was hoping you would be my chief bridesmaid.'

'Oh, that's a real honour,' Lily breathed, going and sitting back on the sofa.

'It's an honour that comes with responsibility,' Goldie said, writing some notes that came to mind about what Lily would have to do. 'Basically, you'll be helping me plan the wedding, and it's usual for the chief bridesmaid to organise a bachelorette party.'

'Do you mean a hen party?' Lily said, clapping her hands gleefully. 'Oh, I love parties. I am so looking forward to that.'

'Thanks, Lily.' Goldie smiled and consulted her notes. 'Rose, I'd like to ask you to be our wedding photographer?'

'I'd love to,' Rose said. 'I've done some weddings before so I'm sure I'll know what you'd like. I like to take some off-the-wall stuff too, you know, unusual angles and backgrounds. What do you say?'

Goldie briefly thought of James. She knew he wanted a very traditional wedding. How would he like off-the-wall shots, whatever they were? She could imagine his expression. She decided she'd worry about that later.

'I say that sounds marvellous,' she said, and was rewarded by Rose's sweet smile.

'What about me?' April said sharply. 'Do I get to share in this group hug?'

'Isn't it obvious what I'd like you to do for me?' Goldie asked gently. 'You make party and celebration cakes for a living. Would you please make us a lovely, fantastic wedding cake?'

Did she detect a slight flush of pleasure on April's cheeks? If so, it passed quickly. April frowned.

'I'll need some deadlines to work to, because I'll need to make a practice cake for you to sample, and to be quite frank, I'm terribly busy. But I daresay I can squeeze you in.'

'Thank you, April. We do appreciate it. I'd much rather have a cake designed by you than a shop-bought one made by a stranger. James will be the same.'

Actually, James had told her he thought they should order a cake from Harrods. Goldie had browsed them online, and they all looked delicious and so beautiful that she was sorely tempted. But she couldn't leave April out of her sharing in the wedding. Besides, April's cakes were to die for, too.

'Let me get this straight,' April said. 'You got engaged at New Year, it's now mid-February, and your wedding is in August. That's only six months from now. I thought every bride needed at least a year to book a venue and plan her wedding.'

'It was a lovely engagement party,' Rose said dreamily. 'James looked so pleased when you said yes.'

'It's a pity Bryce spoilt the moment by slipping on some wine in the kitchen and breaking Dad's favourite crystal decanter,' Lily giggled.

'I'd rather forget that,' Goldie said, shaking her head. 'I don't know who was more mortified, Bryce or your mother. She looked like she wanted to murder him.'

'Knowing Mum, she probably did,' Lily agreed cheerfully. 'She likes her get-togethers choreographed to precision. We know you're good at planning, Goldie, but you're nowhere near Mum's league. Thank goodness.'

'Bryce just laughed,' Rose said. 'I

remember being quite envious of how laid-back he is. He did apologise to you and James, though. He has got manners.'

'Can we not talk about Bryce just now?' Goldie said. 'I'd rather talk about the wedding. To answer your question, April, yes it's a tight schedule, but I know I can handle it. Mr and Mrs Smith kindly gave us a booking for August, and James wants us to have the reception at the Mansion House Hotel. It makes sense, as it's the family business, and it's a beautiful place.'

Everywhere else was booked up for a year, sometimes two years in advance, Goldie reminded herself. They really had no choice but to accept James's parents' offer. She would have preferred somewhere less grand, but that was not to be. Also, she'd have liked somewhere that Mrs Smith didn't have control over. She sighed inwardly.

'Have we finished? I have to go.' April got up and grabbed her smart handbag. 'I'll see you all later.'

When she'd gone, Rose looked at the others. 'It's almost lunch time. Shall we order some of the quiche and salad and a glass of white wine?'

* * *

Later, Goldie went to visit James. She parked her small car on the roadside and went in through the vast outdoor space full of cars and into the salesroom. James had inherited the upmarket car sales business from his father when his parents decided to buy the Mansion House Hotel and run it. He not only sold cars, he rented them out too. Vast Bentleys and polished Rolls sat waiting in the forecourt alongside shiny sports cars and family saloons and the inevitable 'Chelsea tractors'.

She couldn't afford to buy a car here, Goldie thought. Of course, once she married James, she would be very comfortably off. She would finally be part of society in the upper part of

Mayborough. She liked that idea. Not because of the wealth that came with it, but because of the sense of belonging.

She had had such a rootless child-hood, always torn up from any place she began to make friends in. Once she reached her majority at eighteen, she'd said enough was enough. Her parents had been shocked when she refused to move to Germany with them. Once she'd explained, they had readily agreed to pay for her boarding with a local family and for her fees at Mayborough College.

She had never lived with them again. In fact, she'd only seen them on a handful of occasions since then. They were too far away, and it was too expensive to travel to visit them. She'd hoped they might come to her, but their jobs were intense and they had few vacations. Or that was their excuse. She suspected they could have made the effort if they wanted to. Travelling was easy for them; it was their way of life.

'Mr Smith is in his office.' Stella

smiled as Goldie went in.

She thanked the secretary and knocked quietly on the door. James didn't like noise, she knew. When he called out to come in, she pushed open the door but was careful to close it behind her so Stella couldn't overhear them. James didn't like his staff knowing his private business.

'Darling, how lovely to see you,' he said, standing up politely from behind his enormous walnut desk.

He came round and gave her a peck on the cheek. Goldie turned her mouth towards his, but James had already walked away to sit down again. He indicated the chair on the other side of the desk. She sat, feeling deflated in some indescribable way.

'Did you have a nice coffee with the girls?' he asked, tapping at his open laptop and frowning at something on the screen.

'Yes, I did. It's all organised. Lily's agreed to be chief bridesmaid, Rose will take the photos, and April's going to make our cake.'

'Is that wise?' James's eyebrows rose in query.

For a horrible instant, he looked just like his father. Mr Smith had bushy eyebrows and receding grey hair and a thickset frame. Goldie noticed James was getting rather stout. She hoped he wouldn't put on any extra weight after he ordered up his wedding suit.

'Is what wise? Lily has to be chief bridesmaid. She is your sister, after all.'

'Lily, as you well know, is the black sheep of our family. She smoked from the age of fourteen and illegally drove our father's sales cars around the fields at night from the same age. Look at where she's living now and what she does for a job. Heaven help her.'

'Are you saying I shouldn't have made her my bridesmaid? Because it is traditional, and I know that's the kind of wedding you want. We want,' she corrected herself.

James let out a long-suffering sigh. 'Can Rose take a good photograph? We can afford to get a professional photographer, after all.'

'She *is* a professional photographer. That's what she does for a living.'

'I thought she drew pictures for kids' books?'

'She's a children's' book illustrator too. She's very artistic. James . . . I promise you, it'll be fine.' She went round to his side of the desk and kissed the top of his head. She stroked his thinning hair because she knew he liked that.

'I was going to buy the cake. You didn't have to organise that part of our wedding.' His voice was verging on petulant.

'I had to give April a job. I couldn't leave her out of the whole thing.'

'I don't see why not. She's never liked me and has made that plain,' he huffed.

'Nonsense. Of course she likes you. April can be . . . a little prickly, that's all. She's hard to get to know. You have to work at it.'

17

'I don't see why. She's the one with a problem.'

'Well anyway, I got a lot of things sorted this morning and we're on schedule to get married. It's very exciting. Lily had a great idea of having a marquee with a champagne welcome for our guests, and waiters dressed as characters from *My Fair Lady*.'

She watched James visibly wince. 'Darling,' he said, 'I know *My Fair Lady* is your favourite film, but do you really think waiters dressed as chimney sweeps and professors and whatnot is entirely appropriate? I have a position to maintain in Mayborough, especially as I want to become a councillor in due course.'

'It doesn't matter,' Goldie said swiftly. 'Shall we keep the marquee and champagne and ditch the dressing up?'

'Splendid idea.'

She leaned down and in to kiss him on the lips. He jumped back in his chair as if she'd slapped him. 'Not here. What if Stella saw us?' he hissed.

'She'd have to have X-ray eyes then,' Goldie teased, trying to hide her hurt. 'The door's shut, honey, and no one can see in that high window.'

'She might come in to give me my paperwork. We need to be circumspect.'

Goldie bit down on a retort. She knew when she'd accepted James's proposal what he was like. It was part of his charm. He was very . . . *English*. She liked his old-world charm and manners and the way he dressed so smartly. They got on well, and she saw no reason why their marriage wouldn't be perfectly amiable.

'Mother and Dad want us to go over tonight for dinner. You should go home and rest and get freshened up. It will just be the four of us, but they like dinner to be formal. Little black dress and pearls, you know the sort of thing.'

Goldie did know, only too well. Her heart sank. Going to dinner with the Smiths on a Saturday evening was the last thing she wanted to do. She'd hoped to have dinner with James at the

19

new bistro in town. It looked relaxed and inviting. Dinner at the Smiths wasn't going to be that. Now she'd have to go home and try to remember how to use the excessive amounts of cutlery that were bound to be on display at the dining table.

2

It was a sweltering July weekend. Goldie's curls were plastered to her forehead and she pushed them back, wishing for a cool breeze. She was sitting on a bench on Mayborough promenade looking out at a sparkling blue sea. She glanced at her watch. Where was Bryce? She'd made a lunch date with him but he was late.

'Hey! Do you want vanilla and choc or mint and honeycomb?' His familiar deep voice sounded behind her.

Goldie turned and laughed. 'I hope you got some napkins for those, they're melting like crazy.'

'Yeah, well, you just have to eat them quickly. Here you go.'

Bryce pushed a dripping ice cream cone into her hand, followed by a small bundle of tissues. He sat on the bench beside her, and for a moment they didn't try to chat but enjoyed the sweet taste and the beautiful view. Goldie sighed with pleasure as she crunched the last piece of cone.

'That was delicious, thanks. Was that lunch?'

'That wasn't enough? If you insist on being greedy, there's a new place opened on the seafront that does mussels and a seafood platter for two.'

'Mmm, sounds good. Shall we sit here for a minute before we go?'

'Sure. It's nice to get a pause in the day. I've left a great pile of useless sketches in the office that I don't want to see again soon.'

Bryce was an engineer who designed bridges and other infrastructure. He'd won awards for his sleek creations.

'If you're sketching another bridge idea, then I'm sure they aren't useless,' Goldie said. 'Did you get the wedding invitation?'

'You mean, why haven't I answered it? When I got it weeks ago. Sorry, Goldie, you know I wouldn't miss your

22

wedding for the world. I just haven't got around to the formal answering. How's the organising going?'

Goldie looked at him. If Lily, Rose and April were her three best female friends, then Bryce Laidlaw was her best male friend. He'd arrived from Scotland for the final year at high school about the same time she had. They'd had that 'fitting in' experience together, two foreigners in a new land, or so it had felt. With his dark hair and lean build, he hadn't changed much since those school days.

'Your mum told me you were coming to the wedding. I didn't think otherwise.'

'Mum is very excited you're getting married. She's bought her outfit already.' Bryce grinned.

'There was a time when she thought we'd be the ones getting married,' Goldie said with a smile. 'I hope she's not too disappointed.'

'She'll get over it,' Bryce said, throwing his ice-cream-covered tissues into the nearby bin. 'We were never really suited.'

'You didn't think that when we dated at school,' Goldie couldn't help saying. Why it rankled, she didn't know.

'We were kids. It was fun but we broke up, so that tells you something.'

'But we stayed friends, that's what matters.'

'Just as well, with you boarding with us for years. It would have been a nightmare if we'd stopped talking to each other. Mum would've been horri-fied,' Bryce laughed.

'You went to college, so I hardly saw you after that,' Goldie murmured.

'You didn't miss me; you had hundreds of guys after you,' Bryce teased. 'James is one lucky man. I should go and tell him that.'

'Thanks, that's just what he wants to hear. Or rather . . . not. I'm doing all the wedding organisation, but you'd think he was bearing the brunt of it, the way he sighs all the time.' The words came out of Goldie's mouth without filtering, and then she felt ashamed of herself. Bryce was the last person she should be grumbling to about her fiancé. Bryce and James were so different. They'd moved in very different circles at school and managed to avoid each other despite attending the same university. She suddenly felt disloyal.

'Forget I said that,' she said quickly.

'I didn't hear a thing. You never answered my question, though. How's the organising going?'

Goldie shook her head. 'I thought it would be great fun, planning my own wedding. But it's really a lot of work. To get it right, I ought to leave my job and do it full time. I'm worried about Lily, for a start.'

Bryce laughed. 'Worried about Lily? No one worries about Lily; she's the most relaxed and happy person I know. What's the deal?'

'That's the problem. She's being a little too relaxed when it comes to getting stuff done. I keep having to prompt her and push her along, suggest she makes a call or writes a list of what she needs to do. We're talking flowers, favours, table decorations . . . I could go on, but you get the idea. Then I went and asked her if she'd drive James's Bentley to get me to the church and to the reception afterwards. I may have asked for one too many tasks.'

'Don't be daft. If there's one thing Lily loves, it's driving. It'll be great.'

Bryce crossed his long legs and put his arms behind his head, tilting his face to the sun. Goldie had an impulse to scream. Did no one understand how important all this was? Getting married only happened once, if you were lucky. She wanted it to be absolutely perfect. She wanted to make memories that would last a lifetime. She and James should be sitting together when they were old, reminding each other of their gorgeous wedding day.

She nudged him with her elbow. He grunted, eyes shut. 'For goodness sake, Bryce, are you falling asleep on me?'

He opened one eye and gave a lazy grin. Goldie shook her head in exasperation. A couple of young women passed them as they walked along the promenade. Goldie didn't miss how their gazes turned to Bryce as they went by. He was a very attractive man. But he could be very annoying. She kicked his ankle childishly.

'What? Oh, very well, I'll wake up just for you. That sunshine is good stuff. Shall we go and check out the seafood place? I'm getting hungry.' He stood up and stretched.

Goldie tried not to notice how a strip of tanned, muscled stomach showed as his shirt parted from his jeans. He tucked it back in and she was relieved. To cover her confusion, she did what she always did when nervous and began to chat about all and nothing.

Bryce didn't interrupt, and they walked along the seafront to the new restaurant. The sun was pleasantly hot on her bare shoulders. On the beach, children were screaming in delight as they paddled and made sand castles.

Lunch was sensational. Goldie decided she'd come back with the girls. Bryce described his latest bridge project. She deliberately didn't say more about the wedding. It was only later, when she got home, that she realised he hadn't properly explained why he hadn't answered the wedding invitation.

★   ★   ★

Rose was tired. She had been at a christening party all afternoon for a friend's baby boy. It was expected that she'd take photographs of the event. Gill and her husband Alan hadn't formally asked her, but Rose knew they'd be disappointed if she didn't email over some images she'd taken. Baby Zachary was very photogenic, so it wasn't hard to take some good shots. She sometimes wished though, that she could simply go to a celebration or party without taking her camera.

It was now early evening. The sun was still high in a bright blue sky. It felt like early afternoon, were it not for her desire to fall asleep. She was looking forward to getting home to her flat and collapsing on her sofa. She drove along carefully while she thought of switching on the telly and eating popcorn instead of dinner while she watched a romantic comedy.

Parking in the communal car park, she sat for a minute, glad to be back. She lived in a block of modern flats at the top of the town. There was safe parking and nearby shops, with a twenty-four-hour supermarket. That was handy, as Rose often forgot to write a shopping list and had to nip out for biscuits or jam or milk. The view from her third floor window was spectacular as she looked down across Mayborough town to the sea. She spent many happy moments at her living room window, cradling a cup of coffee and enjoying the sight in different seasons and weathers.

29

Rose frowned. She hadn't noticed when she parked, but now she did. There were four policemen at the entrance to the block of flats. How had she missed seeing the police car parked nearby? She'd been too engrossed in her own thoughts.

She got out and locked her car. Then she hurried across to the front doors.

One of the policemen barred her way. 'Hold on, miss. Do you live here?'

'Yes, I do. I live on the third floor, flat Three A.'

'What's your name, love?' he asked kindly.

He was an older man, and he reminded Rose of her father in some way. She still missed her dad so much. He'd passed away a year ago but it felt like less. She rubbed her nose, determined not to cry in front of the police. How embarrassing that would be.

'What's going on?' she asked.

'Your name please.'

'Sorry, I'm Rose Redd. Can I go home now?'

'I'll come up with you. There's been a spate of burglaries here and I'm afraid your flat is one of them.'

'What? Oh no, what have they taken?'

Rose began to run up the stairwell, her camera bag hitting her thigh painfully as she went. The policeman lumbered up after her, panting for breath by the time they reached the third floor.

Rose cried out. Her front door had been kicked in and some of the wood was splintered around the lock and at the bottom. She went in, looking about.

'I need a list of what's been taken,' the policeman said.

'The television for one,' Rose said in dismay.

So much for her plan to watch the telly while dozing. More importantly, had the thief stolen any of her work? She raced into her spare room and gave a huge sigh of relief. Her design board was there with the illustrations for the current project pinned to it. They hadn't been vandalised or tampered with. These were the most important items she owned. She could replace the television, but not these.

'Anything else missing?'

'I don't know. I'll check.'

She heard him sit heavily on her sofa, its old frame creaking. She checked her bedside cabinet, her sock drawer and other places where her valuables resided. It was a relief that she didn't own much of value, she thought wryly. Her camera equipment was of most monetary value, costing into the thousands, but it went everywhere with her. She sent up a silent prayer of thanks that she'd taken it to baby Zachary's christening that day, after all.

She went back through into the living room. The policeman was mopping his brow with a white handkerchief. It was hot in the room as the sun streamed in. Rose went over and opened the window. He nodded gratefully.

'Whoever it was has taken some money — not more than a hundred pounds that I'd foolishly left in my drawer, and some jewellery that wasn't worth much but which I liked.'

'That and the television, nothing else?' He wrote something in his notebook.

Rose shook her head. 'I don't have much that anyone would want to steal, to be honest. Luckily I had my camera out with me today. Was mine the only flat to be broken into?'

'He had time to break into your neighbour's and one upstairs on the fourth floor too.'

'Will he come back?' Rose asked.

The policeman heaved himself up. 'Very unlikely. It's an opportunistic crime, probably youngsters. Thankfully we don't see much of this in Mayborough. You've been unlucky, Miss Redd, I'm sorry to say. I'd advise you to get your door boarded up tonight and get better locks. We may be in touch at some point for a further statement from you. Good day.'

He let himself out, and Rose was

33

left in her flat. She sat on the sofa and found that her legs were trembling. She got up and made a pot of coffee. The weather was more suited to lemonade, but she felt chilled despite the heat. The coffee warmed her. She knew she had to phone the locksmith. The policeman's tone had been a little disapproving when he mentioned her lock. It was true, she'd only had one. She never thought her flat would get broken into. She lived in such a nice part of town. Rose decided to ask the locksmith for two good strong locks and a bolt.

After the joiner had brought a new, good quality door and the locksmith had added the security she needed, Rose made popcorn in her microwave and another pot of coffee. She took her food over to the sofa. She had no telly to watch, so she read some magazines instead.

She went to bed early, exhausted from the day. She dreamt that she was at a party, blowing up colourful balloons. Her dream-self skipped through a green meadow, releasing the balloons, which floated up into a cloudless sky. Then it changed. A dark shadow loomed over her and all the balloons popped. In her dream, she screamed and ran. Rose sat bolt upright in her bed. Her fingers gripped the duvet, twisting the cotton. She was sweating.

Her bedroom was pitch black. She wished she hadn't shut the door. What if someone was in her flat? What if he was creeping towards her bedroom right now? She tried not to make a sound. She listened for movement. Nothing. Silently, she slipped from her bed and tiptoed to the door. She paused. Then she flung it open, ready to yell for help.

There was no one there. Feeling foolish, yet with her heart pounding in her chest, Rose checked every inch of her home to make sure she was alone. Then she went back and sat in her bed, leaving the door open. She didn't lie down and she didn't shut her eyes. She kept vigil under the small hours, when her body gave way and she fell asleep without knowing it.

★ ★ ★

'What don't you understand? I simply need another cake. And I need it pronto,' April snapped.

Sally, who baked the cakes, looked puzzled. 'What's wrong with the one I gave you?'

'It crumbled on one edge. That meant the icing wasn't smooth; and in turn, that means I can't set up the decorations the way they have to be. Just get me another cake, please.'

'You're the boss,' Sally said in that infuriating way she had of making April feel small and not at all the boss, but more of a nuisance.

'Yes, Sally, I am the boss, and I'm sure I don't need to remind you of that. We'll all be more efficient if we can remember it and get on with our work.

This cake has to be sent before six p.m. by courier, so let's get on with what we have to do.'

Sally looked as if she'd wanted say something else before she firmly shut her mouth and went out. April brought out the cake she'd been working on. She'd hidden it before asking Sally to come in. There was nothing wrong with the cake itself. There was no crumbly edge. She'd lied.

April picked up the fondant piping tool again. The cake already had half its fondant pleats and ruffles in place. But they weren't right. She held the piping tool over the smooth icing. Before she could start, her hands began to shake. With a muffled cry, she flung the tool down. What was wrong with her?

She pushed the damaged cake into a cupboard as she heard Sally approach. Her assistant smiled nicely as she put a new cake onto April's worktop.

'There you go, fingers crossed this one is perfect. It should be. I'm sorry, April, I have no idea why the last one crumbled. It won't happen again.'

April wasn't so sure. If her hands kept shaking the way they had been the last couple of days, there were going to be more mistakes and more excuses to be made. What on earth was she to do? Her cake making and decorating business was her life. She made to order and sent cakes all over the country. She also had a thriving online order website. How was she going to deliver cakes to the high standard she herself had set if there was something wrong with her?

She wished briefly for someone to talk to. Lily, Rose or Goldie? No. It wasn't fair to burden Goldie with her problems when she was busy with her wedding. April couldn't imagine telling Rose her innermost fears, and as for Lily . . . what advice was she going to give?

Her shoulders went back and she stiffened her spine. She'd manage. Just the way she always managed. On her own.

3

Lily lived outside of Mayborough, in a wooden cabin in a lush green valley. Goldie took a winding country road, fringed with birch and willow and tussocks of wildflowers. She knew where Lily's cabin was, but usually got lost on the way there. Perhaps because she didn't visit often. Usually, Lily came into town when they all met up.

There were two cats sunning themselves in the yard as Goldie's car drew up. She stroked the black and white cat with no tail, remembering when Lily had rescued him from the railway track as a stray. The ginger torn stared at her with accusing yellow eyes, then slunk away round the corner of the cabin. She glanced about. There was a stack of firewood against the side of the cabin. There were scattered clay pots of flowers; red and pink geraniums, delicate pink and white dancing ladies and others she didn't know with yellow blooms. Lily's ancient camper van squatted beyond them, its faded blue paint even shabbier than she remembered.

That campervan held a lot of memories. Goldie found herself smiling as she looked at it. When they were all eighteen, they had gone on a tour of Europe in it and had a wonderful, wild time seeing the sights and ticking off countries. And laughing a lot. An awful lot. They'd been young and foolish and full of joy. She sighed wistfully. Those days seemed a long time ago.

Near to the campervan was another vehicle. A yellow minibus stood gleaming with some soap suds still dripping from the wheel rims. Lily was a bus driver for the private boarding school in Mayborough which involved ferrying pupils around, often to the airport at term breaks to visit their parents. Goldie had never been able to determine Lily's working hours, as they were quite haphazard.

The cabin door opened and Lily stood there grinning. Her long skirts were sopping wet and she was drying her hands on a piece of tea towel.

'Goldie, hello. I wasn't expecting you. Or was I? Did we make an arrangement? Anyway, come on in.'

Goldie pushed her sunglasses onto her hair and followed Lily inside. The room smelt of seasoned wood and patchouli. There were books everywhere. On the windowsill there was a vase of wildflowers and a driftwood branch with silvery-green lichen. A low couch was draped in a gold and red sari.

'Have a seat,' Lily offered, indicating the couch.

Goldie eyed the enormous grey cat with tattered ears taking up much of the space, and the spilled pile of books that took up the rest. She sat instead on the bamboo chair near the window.

'Sorry, I'll have to leave you for a moment and get changed. I've been

41

washing the minibus; I'm needed tomorrow on a school trip.'

'What's that?' Goldie said sharply. She pointed at a cardboard box on the table which was quivering.

Lily reached over and carefully opened the flaps. 'Have a look.'

Cautiously, Goldie peered in. A small mess of feathers shifted and she saw a beady eye stare back at her.

'As I said, what's that?'

'This is Rowena. She's a baby crow. She fell out of the trees in the back garden, and the parents couldn't get her back into the nest, so I've taken over. I'm feeding her cat food and she's loving it.'

'Rowena?'

Lily grinned. 'She can't just be 'crow', can she? I'll leave you two to get better acquainted while I get some dry clothes.'

Goldie sat quite still, waiting for Lily. She hoped that Rowena wasn't going to suddenly fly up out of the box. She didn't really like birds. Besides, how would the grey cat react to a small bird loose in the room? It didn't bear thinking about.

Lily looked surprised to see her still there. She was wearing yet another long cotton skirt and was barefoot.

'I thought you'd have put the kettle on. What do want, coffee or tea? I've got cinnamon, fruit spice or peppermint.'

'Peppermint tea, please.'

She waited while Lily hummed a tune and produced two chipped mugs with real peppermint leaves in them.

'I see the campervan is still on the go,' Goldie said, sipping her tea.

'Of course,' Lily laughed. 'There's years left in it. There are more adventures to be had.'

'We had some good times, didn't we?'

'Some great times,' Lily said. 'Do you remember the tractor I borrowed?'

Goldie shuddered. 'How could I forget it.'

That was the night of The Incident.

The night that Goldie suddenly grew up. Yet to Lily, it was just some teenage high jinks.

'I'm amazed we got away with that. Farmer Bow never found out who took it joy riding.'

'Lily! We were lucky not to be killed that night. I don't know why you find it so amusing.'

'It wasn't that serious. I knew how to drive it.'

'And that's why we narrowly missed hitting a tree and ended up in the middle of a hay field?' Goldie's voice rose.

Lily laughed. 'You should see your face. Honestly, Goldie, you need to lighten up. You're turning into an old fuddy duddy, like James. In fact, have you ever told James about our tractor adventure?' Her eyes were alight with mischief.

Goldie pushed back her chair. 'You must never, I mean *never*, tell James that I was involved in that. Do you hear me? He'd . . . He'd . . . I don't know what he'd do. James has ambitions to be a councillor, and I have to be the most respectable of wives. Promise me you won't say a word.'

Lily raised her hands in surrender. 'Okay, I promise. But I don't know what the big deal is. You were young and having fun. No one died, and Farmer Bow's tractor didn't get any damage. It was worth it to drive that machine. I'd love to drive another one.'

'Let's just . . . leave this conversation, shall we? Anyway, I came to find out how you're getting on with the wedding.'

Lily took a long swig of her tea and set the mug down. 'It's fine.'

'Fine?'

'Yeah, fine. More tea?' Lily got up and gathered up the mugs with an enquiring expression.

'No. No, thanks. My wedding? Can we talk about this, please?'

Lily sat down again. 'What do you want to know?'

'Well, everything! It's only a little

over a month to go until the big day. Have you organised the flowers? What about the favours? Am I having a bachelorette party?'

Goldie rummaged in her bag and brought out her notebook and pen. She saw Lily glance at them. Well that was too bad. Lily wasn't one for lists and being organised. But a wedding absolutely needed that attention to detail. She took the top of her pen, ready to write.

'Let's start with the bachelorette party. Have you booked anything? Who have you invited? Do I need to wear anything special? Will we be travelling far?'

She wrote 'bachelorette party' and a large question mark in her notebook and looked up at Lily.

Lily shook her head. 'No, I'm not telling you. It's meant to be a surprise.'

'But you *have* organised it?'

Lily rubbed at her nose and said nothing. Goldie waved her notebook and raised her eyebrows. *Come on,*

Lily, answer me.

'Has anyone ever told you that it's possible to be too organised?' Lily said.

'Yes, but I don't believe it. Are you going to answer my question or not?'

'Not. But you can ask about other stuff, if you like.'

'Moving on to the flowers, then. Have you sorted those out?'

'I spoke to Davey at Mayborough Flowers and gave him some ideas.'

'But have you confirmed what we need?'

'Will you stop?' Lily stood up. 'Seriously, you need to stop hassling me. If you're worried about the flowers, why don't you speak to Davey.'

'Right then, I will.'

'Anyway, I'm not sure the flowers are the chief bridesmaid's duty. Or the favours. I think you're meant to do them. I'm doing the hen party and I'm supposed to help you look for a wedding dress.'

'Oh.'

There was an awkward silence.

Goldie stuffed her notebook back in her bag. Maybe she was expecting too much of Lily.

'I've got my wedding dress already.'

'You have?'

'Yes, I bought it back in March. I'm sorry, I never thought to ask you to come with me to choose it. I suppose I knew exactly what I wanted.'

'I don't mind,' Lily said. 'I'm glad you got the dress you wanted.'

'I'll do the favours too,' Goldie said. 'I'll leave the bachelorette . . . hen party to you. What about driving the Bentley?'

'In my bridesmaid dress? Even for me, that would be a challenge.'

'I never thought of that,' Goldie groaned. 'I can't believe I didn't think of that. What's the matter with me?'

'Nothing's the matter except wedding-itis. What about Bryce? He could be the chauffeur.'

'That's a great idea. I'll ask him today.'

'Goldie?'

'What?'

'Are you sure about this?'

'I don't know what you mean.'

Goldie got up and grabbed her bag. She had to be in the office in the afternoon, having taken the morning off for wedding business.

'You know, marrying my brother? Are you sure he's the one?'

'Of course I'm sure,' Goldie said. 'Why on earth are you asking me that?'

Lily shrugged. Beside her on the table, Rowena rattled her box and let out a thin cheep. The grey cat twitched an ear but didn't wake up.

'What about Bryce?'

'Bryce is my friend. It's James that I'm marrying. And yes, I'm sure he's the one, as you put it. Now, I have to go. I'm due in to work in half an hour.'

She hurried out of the cabin with its sweet scents and odd animals, passing the camper van on her way. She looked in the rear view mirror as she drove off. Lily stood staring at her, framed by the wooden door, her cats at her feet.

After work, she was due at the Smiths' for dinner. She made a special effort with her dress and put on a favourite necklace. Her makeup was understated but perfect, and she put her hair up, the way James liked it.

James was at his parents' home when she arrived. She felt a slight annoyance at that. Shouldn't they have arrived together? As it was, she felt very much the outsider as she followed the maid into the living room to find the three of them there. Their home was part of the Mansion House Hotel, a wing of it on the third floor.

'Mr and Mrs Smith, lovely to see you. James.' Goldie smiled politely at his parents and warmed her smile for him.

'Darling, you look quite lovely.' James moved forward to kiss her on the cheek.

Behind him, his parents managed civilised smiles. Goldie was very aware that they disapproved of James's choice of bride. They'd wanted someone with wealth and connections. She was a disappointment. She had no money and she wasn't even English.

'I think perhaps we might reduce the formalities now that you're marrying James,' Mr Smith said. 'Do call us Margery and Hugh.'

'Thank you.' Goldie forced back a laugh with difficulty. This was like the Victorian age. Could they be any stuffier?

'Let's go through for our meal, shall we?' Margery said. 'We're sampling your wedding menu tonight, so do pay full attention to what you're eating.'

'You didn't tell me that,' Goldie whispered to James.

Her annoyance went up a notch to anger, maybe even fury. How dare they! She hadn't been asked about the menu yet at all. She'd imagined that she'd organise that very soon with the hotel. Now it looked as if she'd have no say over it at all.

'Do speak up, darling. I can hardly hear you.' He waited until his parents had gone into the dining room ahead of them and then grabbed her arm. 'Don't make a fuss, please, Goldie. My mother has arranged this meal specially for you.'

'You're hurting my arm. Let me go.'

He released his grip and Goldie rubbed her arm. She didn't know what to think. Why was James taking his mother's side? Where was his loyalty to Goldie? Could he not see why she was upset?

She slid into her seat, and the maid hurried forward with the starter dishes. She barely tasted the food. The conversation was dull as James talked about the car sales business and his plans for expansion.

'James tells me you like looking at the stars,' Hugh Smith said to Goldie.

He might as well have said she liked throwing chicken entrails and reading the signs, she thought, from his tone.

'Yes, I love star gazing, it's my hobby,' she said, spearing an out of season asparagus and forcing it down.

'I can't understand the attraction

myself,' he said, shaking his head and pouring himself more wine.

'Well, it's actually really fascinating . . . '

'You won't have much time for hobbies once you're James's wife,' he interrupted her. 'Isn't that a fact, Margery?'

'Every important man needs a supportive wife behind him,' Margery said, nodding. 'You have to put aside your little pursuits and make sure your husband has everything he needs.'

'Isn't that attitude, like, out of the nineteen fifties?' Goldie smirked, looking about to share the joke.

She saw three stony faces. She looked back at her asparagus, wilting in a pool of butter. She consoled herself that James wasn't quite so stuffy away from his parents. Everyone reverted a little to childhood behaviours when they went back home, she thought. She just had to get James to herself and persuade him they could do things differently.

'Have you thought about where you

want to live after you get married?'
Margery was asking.

Now, Goldie had thought quite a bit
about that. James currently lived in a
new apartment in Mayborough town
centre but she'd been looking at some
beautiful houses overlooking the sea, a
few miles out of town. They had big,
leafy gardens and quiet locales but with
only a short commute to work.

So she was horrified to hear Hugh
begin to speak directly to James, not
turning to her at all.

'Your mother and I have an idea we
want to run past you. Now that Granny
Headon is no longer with us, the
dowager flat is empty. It's spacious and
it has a linking corridor to the rest of
the Mansion House. What do you
think? It could be our wedding gift to
you.'

'That's very generous, isn't it,
Goldie?' James said, turning to her,
pink with pleasure.

That was it? He wasn't going to
discuss it with her? He was making a

huge decision that affected both of them, just like that. Goldie swallowed an urge to scream.

'It's very generous,' she said, 'but we haven't talked about where we'll live after we get married yet. We might want to move out of town.'

Out of town and away from the influence of Margery and Hugh. James was a better person away from his parents. He was livelier and more fun. And more affectionate too.

'Out of town? Why would you do that?' Margery asked. She waved at the maid, who began to clear the dishes and bring in the desserts.

'There are some lovely houses which would be great to raise a family in,' Goldie said.

There was a frosty silence, broken only by the maid setting down the dishes of meringues and fresh strawberries.

'We don't want to live out of town,' James said firmly, not catching Goldie's gaze. 'We've no plans to have a family for a good long while, and we'd love to take up your kind offer of the dowager flat. Wouldn't we, Goldie?'

She was trapped. Her heart beat like a caged bird and her hand shook a little as she spooned up the fruit. If she wanted to marry James, it looked like she had to accept some decisions she didn't like. What was that about not wanting to have a family? They hadn't exactly talked about having children, but Goldie had assumed they both wanted them. Now, she was hearing James say he didn't want any right now. When did he want them, then? She burned to ask him, but there was no way she could say anything with his parents there.

'Goldie?'

'Yes, it's a very kind offer,' she said through numb lips.

She managed to get through the rest of dinner quietly seething.

'What did you think of the menu?' Margery asked her.

Goldie was actually surprised to be

asked her opinion of anything.

'It was nice,' she said.

'Nice? Is that a recommendation? If you don't like it, just say. I can have another meal tomorrow night for you and James to sample.'

'No, really, it was very nice. We don't need a different menu,' Goldie said hastily.

There was no way she could sit through another meal so soon. It struck her then that she was doomed to spend the rest of her life having family dinners with Margery and Hugh. Perhaps they'd grow to love her or at least to accept her, she thought. Surely, once she and James were married, they'd be less judgemental of her.

'James likes good food,' Margery went on. 'It's up to you to make sure he gets wholesome, traditional meals. Are you giving up your job once you're married?'

'No, I've no intention of giving up my job.'

'You won't need to work. James

57

makes more than enough to keep you both in comfort. Does he know you intend to work?'

James and his father had by now moved through to the living room with their drinks. Goldie heard their similar voices. There was no laughter, no teasing, but serious discussion. Of what, she couldn't make out. Probably car sales or how the hotel was doing. She thought longingly of her own tiny flat, with its balcony and her telescope waiting for her to watch the night sky. How early could she leave? Being high summer, it was still light, but she didn't mind waiting up til very late to catch the stars.

'We haven't discussed my work,' she told Margery. *Just as we haven't discussed children or where we'll live.* The two women moved through to the living room to join the men.

4

'Lily suggested that I ask you to drive the Bentley,' Goldie said.

She and Bryce were standing on her balcony looking out at a perfect velvet-black sky sprinkled with glittering stars. The telescope was angled up and Bryce's face pressed up against it. His voice was muffled as he answered.

'I'm flattered.'

'She could hardly manage it in her bridesmaid dress,' Goldie shook her head. 'I still can't understand why I couldn't see that. For all my planning, I missed that one.'

Bryce detached himself from the telescope and stood up, rubbing his neck. 'Why don't they make telescopes taller?'

'Because most people aren't as tall as you. You could reduce its height and sit down, you know.'

'Really? Why didn't you tell me that years ago? I've got a permanent kink in my neck because of your star gazing,' he teased.

'Did you see the north star? Isn't it wonderful? So bright and clear tonight. And . . . ' Goldie took Bryce's place at the telescope, her wedding forgotten for a brief moment. ' . . . If I adjust this a tiny bit . . . wait for it . . . you can just make out the Andromeda Galaxy.'

She stood up triumphantly, her eyes flashing with excitement. Okay, she'd seen the Andromeda Galaxy a million times before, but that never diminished the wonder of it. A whole other galaxy filled with trillions of stars and planets. Wow. Was there someone on one of those planets staring through a telescope at the distant Milky Way Galaxy and at her? That kind of thought was thrilling.

'Do you still need a chauffeur?' Bryce asked.

Goldie's focus swung round to her wedding. Apart from the night sky, it was all she thought about these days. Time was ticking away. It made her chest tighten. There was so much to do and not enough days left.

'James wants us to hire someone.'

After the awful dinner with Hugh and Margery, Goldie had waited a couple of days before suggesting lunch with James. They'd met in a Scandinavian-style cafe on the water-front. The place was quite new, and Goldie loved the fresh blond wood furniture and simple designs. She arrived first and ordered a glass of orange juice. She was sitting enjoying the sea view when James arrived.

'Darling,' he said, hurrying over and kissing her cheek.

'That was daring.'

'What?' he looked puzzled, poised to sit.

'Kissing me in public,' Goldie joked. 'Someone might see.' She was still upset about the dinner with his parents and wanted to needle him slightly.

He flushed. 'Don't be silly, darling. I

can kiss my wife-to-be, surely?'

She took pity on him. 'Of course. Don't mind me, you're right. I'm being silly. I've missed us getting together the last two days.'

'I've been very busy at work. Anyway, you don't want to hear about that. What shall we order?'

Goldie waited until the waitress had brought over two menus and taken James's drink order.

'Is everything all right at work?'

'Yes, yes. Nothing to worry about. Sales have been down this week, but I'm sure it's a blip. Now, what about the fish? Shall we order that?'

He didn't want to talk about it. Well, that was okay. She didn't find his work interesting at all. He never asked her how her work was going, either. Goldie was personal assistant to the manager of a white goods firm. She didn't find her own work exciting, but it paid the bills. The echo of Margery's words came back to her. *You won't need to work. James makes more than enough to keep you both.*

It was tempting. She could give up her job and become a lady of leisure. But what would she do with her time? She couldn't imagine being the sort of woman who went to charity lunches and became president of something or other just to fill her days. Besides, her job gave her some independence. And that was important. Her gut instinct told her that.

'Penny for them?' James smiled.

'Just thinking about the favours. Whether I got the right samples. Here, look.'

She dug in her handbag and brought out two small bags. James peered at them dutifully.

'And these are . . . ?'

'This one is five almonds in a gold tracery pouch. The other one is coloured almonds in a red silk pouch. Not much difference. What was I thinking? I should've got the champagne chocolates. They were so cute, shaped like hearts and wrapped in different coloured foil.'

James's warm hand covered hers. She felt a flicker of attraction and turned her palm so she could hold his fingers in hers. Surprisingly, he didn't pull away even when the waitress returned with their plates of hot salmon salad. Instead, he moved so their hands interlaced under the table.

This was James at his best, Goldie thought. This was the man she wanted to marry. Not the stiff upper-class man who appeared when his parents were around. He had a softer, caring side to him that she just had to bring out more.

'I don't care which favours you choose. The main thing is we're getting married,' he said.

'Do you think your parents will ever come round to that?'

'Look, I'm sorry about the other night. I realise I didn't include you in the decision about where to live. But it was difficult, and Mum and Dad did make us a very generous offer. I couldn't turn it down without hurting their feelings.'

What about my *feelings?* Goldie thought. She took a mouthful of the delicious salmon and rocket before answering. She wasn't being fair on him. He did have to consider his parents too.

'Mum and Dad will come to love you as much as I do,' James went on. 'When they see how happy I am once we're married, they'll realise you're good for me.'

'Would you like to go and see the houses I picked out? Just in case you change your mind.'

James shook his head. 'I think the decision is made. Besides, it'll be very convenient living at the Mansion House. We can use the maid service and have meals brought from the dining room. You won't have to do any housework.'

What would there be to do? Goldie's throat closed in sudden panic, and she had to take a sip of orange juice to make the salmon go down without choking her. In her dreams, she'd imagined setting up home together. That meant all the mundane stuff too. The vacuuming, the dusting and tidying of items they bought together that held memories. She'd seen herself cooking lovely meals for James. Or, even better, they'd cook together.

But the way he described it sounded so clinical. She'd live in a house she hadn't chosen and have maids take care of it. To some women, that might sound heavenly not doing the housework, but to Goldie it sounded bad.

'You don't look too happy. Everything all right?' James frowned at her, spearing a bunch of rocket and popping it into his mouth.

She watched him chew. She felt as if everything was out of her control. As if she was a puppet going through actions while someone else pulled her strings. The only thing she could control was her wedding. She could at least do that well.

'Everything is fine,' she said with a firm smile. 'By the way, what do you think about asking Bryce to be our chauffeur for the wedding?'

James blew out a sigh and put his cutlery down. He mopped at his mouth with the napkin and set that down neatly too.

'I don't understand why you want to rope all your acquaintances in to work at the wedding. I've set a very generous budget and we can afford to hire in.'

'They're not my acquaintances, they're my friends. I hope that they'll become your friends too. Lily's your sister, for goodness sake. She, Rose, April and Bryce are like family to me. I love the idea that my friends can be part of something that's so very important to me.'

'Do they actually want to do all this? Are you sure they wouldn't rather simply attend the wedding reception like everyone else?'

Goldie was hurt. Of course her friends wanted to contribute. It made the whole wedding special. James was taking the shine off her ideas. She turned down the waitress's offer of dessert and asked for a black coffee.

'I think they do want to be a part of it. But if you'd rather hire a chauffeur, then I'll go with that.'

James looked satisfied. 'That's the best solution, darling. Trust me. I'm sure Bryce would rather prop up the bar at the wedding instead of driving us about.'

Maybe he was right. It wasn't fair to ask Bryce to forgo the champagne so he could drive them away afterwards. She was beginning to doubt her own judgement.

'Do you want to share my paradise slice?' James asked, pushing his plate towards her.

'Thanks, honey.' She grinned at him.

She needed James's sensible personality to balance her impulses. They were good together, she had to remember that. Once they were married, she'd find a way to tell him they didn't need a maid or ready-made meals. She'd be a proper wife to him and make the dowager apartment into a real home.

Now, shivering a little in the summer night, Goldie watched Bryce stare through the telescope. Even more stars had come out, and the Milky Way was visible as a misty white haze above. The night sky put everything into perspective. She was a tiny dot in a vast universe, and her problems were tiny too.

'Would you have liked to be the chauffeur?' she asked before she could stop herself.

Bryce ducked out of the telescope and glanced over at her. He was wearing his old battered leather jacket and casual jeans. The light from her living room cast his face in angles and planes.

'Sure, I'd have driven you to your wedding. It's not often one gets to drive a Bentley.'

'It's just . . . I realise you wouldn't have been able to have a drink because of driving us away afterwards. I was being selfish.'

Bryce's eyebrows rose. 'You're not a selfish person, Goldie. I'd have been delighted to be your chauffeur. I'm flattered you asked.'

'Are you disappointed then that we're hiring in?'

Bryce laughed. It was a rich sound that warmed Goldie's heart. Honestly, she was all over the place these days. She'd no idea if she was doing well or not.

He pulled her close and hugged her. Goldie reminded herself he was her friend. It was nothing more. So why did it make her feel so good to be held tightly by him? He was warm and solid and she felt so very safe with him. She felt a sense of loss when he put her from him.

'Come on, where's your coffee pot? Let's grab a couple of mugs; I'm getting cold out here. And then you can tell me all your worries and I'll put them out like a light. How about that?'

'That sounds great,' Goldie said gratefully.

★   ★   ★

Rose was at Lily's place. The big grey cat was purring on her lap while the ginger torn and black and white cat sat on the windowsill watching her. She'd brought photos of her book illustrations to show Lily.

'These are great,' Lily said, looking through them. 'I love the haunted woodland with all the little creatures hidden in the branches. Kids will enjoy seeing if they can find them all, won't they?'

'That's the idea,' Rose said, stroking the grey cat's ears and making him purr even more loudly. 'The book's a modern fairy tale, and I absolutely adore working with the author. She's very open to ideas. Some of them have a fixed notion of what they want for the illustrations, but Dorey Stephens has such imagination.'

'You're working with Dorey Stephens? She must be one of the top children's authors by now. They televised one of her books, didn't they?'

Rose nodded. 'She's well known and very gifted.'

'And so are you,' Lily said loyally. 'Otherwise she wouldn't have chosen you to do the artwork. Talking of fairy tales, how's your mum?'

Rose's mother lived in London and worked in the toy department of a large shopping complex. She loved fairy stories so much she'd named her daughter after a fairy tale character.

'Oh, you know Mum. She's full of her usual wonderful and wacky projects. She's decided to take up tapestry, and she's going to create a Bayeux-style banner for her living room. Except instead of battle scenes, it's going to be fairy stories.'

'That's great,' Lily said. 'I can't wait to see it. Can we go and visit?'

Rose laughed. 'She hasn't started her

'how to' class yet. So, it's going to be a while. I know she can do it, but I don't think we need to book our train tickets just yet. Give it a year.'

Lily grinned, 'The best thing about your mum is she never gives up.'

'That's true,' Rose said, feeling the comfort of the cat's soft fur under her fingers. 'Even when Dad died, she kept going for both of us. I'm very lucky she's my mum.'

'You miss him, don't you?' Lily said quietly.

She moved over and hugged her friend. Rose tried to stop the tears welling up in her eyes. Yes, she missed her dad terribly. Perhaps that was why she hadn't been down to London for months. She kept making excuses, saying her work was too busy. But in reality, she couldn't face visiting Mum and feeling Dad's absence in their cosy home. She was a coward.

She was even more cowardly than that, Rose thought, hating herself. She was terrified to sleep at night now after the burglary. Her nightmares came without fail, and she'd wake up screaming or damp with sweat, the sheets tangled around her.

'Lily . . . ' she began, then stopped.

Somehow she couldn't bring herself to confide in Lily about it. Lily's home was so bright and lovely. Every space had an interesting ornament or piece of nature. There were colourful throws and cushions and then of course there were Lily's strays. As for Lily, she was such a happy-go-lucky person. Could she really understand the depth of Rose's dark terror?

Even if Lily understood, Rose couldn't do that to her. She knew that Lily would feel her pain as if it were her own. Then, instead of Rose feeling better, Lily would only feel worse. Rose couldn't, *wouldn't* taint this peaceful place with that.

'Lily,' she said again, 'can I have a coffee, please?'

'What an awful hostess I am.' Lily bounded up with a grin. 'What flavour?

I've got caramel or cinnamon.'

'I'll try cinnamon, please. I'd no idea cinnamon coffee existed.' Rose tried to lighten up. If she focused on Lily and the green leaves brushing the windows outside, surely she'd banish the darkness?

'I brought some photo samples that I'm going to give to Goldie,' she called through to Lily, who was banging something metal in the kitchen.

'Do you have to?' Lily shouted back.

'Have to what?'

Lily reappeared with an ancient coffee pot, two mugs and a painted jug of milk. 'Goldie wants you to do the wedding photography. She doesn't need samples of your work to know you'll do a good job.'

'It wasn't so much Goldie I was thinking about.'

'Ahhh, you mean my big brother.' Lily poured the coffee, thick and black, into the mugs and splashed in some milk. She pushed one over to Rose. 'You mustn't worry about James. He'll come round to what Goldie wants, eventually. Besides, you've nothing to worry about; you take amazing shots. Can I see them?'

Rose unzipped her folder and spread the pictures out on the table. The grey cat stalked off her knee, annoyed at being slightly squashed.

'Sorry, Humphrey,' Rose said, stroking his departing back. To Lily, she said, 'I know Goldie wants us all involved in the wedding, but does James? Goldie is quite evasive when I ask her about him. Do you know what's going on?'

Lily sighed. 'My brother is very traditional. I can imagine he'd like to book the whole wedding through a professional organisation down to the last detail. He's not big on quirkiness. Anyway, don't waste your time worrying about him. Seriously, this wedding is going to be fun. We'll give Goldie our best send off into married life possible.'

'It must be wonderful to be in love and find your soul mate,' Rose said dreamily.

Lily sighed again, this time longer. 'I know, wouldn't it. I haven't even dated for about a year.'

'Me neither,' Rose said, 'I never seem to meet any decent men. This town's too small.'

'Agreed. There's always dating agencies though.'

'Oh, I couldn't.' Rose shook her head, 'I want it to be romantic. I want to lock eyes across a crowded room and fall in love at first sight.'

'Me too. That's dating agencies out, then,' Lily laughed.

She picked up the photos that Rose had laid out and stared at them.

'What's the matter?' Rose asked after some minutes of silence, 'Don't you like them?'

'No, no, I do,' Lily said hurriedly, putting them back in the folder. 'They're a little different from your usual style, that's all. More edgy, I think. Lots of shadows and hints of figures hiding. Almost as if you're photographing fairy tales, but the grim ones. Sorry, Rose, maybe that's not what you want to hear. I'm not sure these will show James what you can do at a wedding.'

5

Rose checked the door before unlocking it. She looked for any signs of damage, any scoring around the locks, any scuffle or kick marks at bottom of the door. With relief, she saw nothing. Looking over her shoulder to check she was alone, she hurried inside her flat and shut the door. Then she slid the chain on. The new door had a peephole. She'd insisted on that. She stared through it now. Nothing. Okay, she could finally relax.

She sat at her low table and spread out the offending photos. Lily was right; there was something ominous about them. Which was strange. She hadn't set out to create a dark, creepy atmosphere. She'd simply wanted to showcase her art for James. To persuade him that she could do a great job of photographing the wedding.

Why hadn't she noticed how bad these were?

She was going to have to start all over again. This time, she'd concentrate on flowers and birds and the shiny, bright seaside. She'd use colour instead of black and white. She might also ask Lily to model for her.

With these positive ideas in mind, Rose stood up and took her camera bag. She made sure to check the peephole before going out and locking up behind her. She was intending to go down the steps and into the communal gardens at the back of the flats, but before she knew what she was doing, her finger was pressing her next-door neighbour's door bell.

She was almost happy when no one answered, but as she turned away, the door was slowly opened. Mrs Dawson's cautious face looked out.

'What do you want?'

Rose's neighbour looked ready to slam the door, and Rose didn't blame her.

'I live next door. I'm Rose.'

'Yes, I know you. You brought me some groceries last winter when there was the terrible snow.' Mrs Dawson opened her door more widely.

'It's . . . it's about the burglary,' Rose said, the words sticking in her throat. 'I got broken into, and I think you did too?'

'You'd better come in.'

Rose followed Mrs Dawson in. She was a tiny bird-like woman with a head of shiny white curls, and blue eyes that reminded Rose of a sunny sea.

'Would you like a cup of tea, dear?'

'No, thanks, Mrs Dawson.'

'It's about the burglary, you said?' Mrs Dawson looked at her in expectation.

Rose shook her head. 'I'm sorry, I'm not quite sure why I came here.'

'You're still worried about the break-in and you're not sleeping well,' Mrs Dawson said with a small smile.

'That's it. How did you know?'

Mrs Dawson laughed. It was a thin,

chirpy sound that reinforced the image of a bird, Rose thought. She was like a sparrow or a robin.

'I know, dear, because I feel exactly the same. When my Stanley came to fix the door, he said to me, Mum you can't stay here on your own after this. And I said to him, whyever not?'

'You did?' Rose whispered.

Mrs Dawson nodded vigorously, making her curls bounce like a halo. 'I did, indeed. No young whippersnapper is going to force me out of my home. I don't mean Stanley, of course. Dear Stanley wanted me to come and live with him and Sandra. But you know, they have three very lively children and two noisy dogs, so I couldn't do that. And I won't give in to bullies. That's what these young thugs want. I won't stand for it.'

Rose stared at her. The image of a dear little robin melted away. Mrs Dawson seemed to grow in stature as she spoke. She was made of steel. Underneath the old-lady veneer, there was strength and determination. She made Rose feel weak and foolish.

'Even though you don't sleep well?' Rose said.

'Even though,' Mrs Dawson said firmly. 'Everything passes with time, dear. Your nightmares will fade too. You've got good locks on your door now?'

'I have four sturdy locks,' Rose said. 'I've got a chain inside and a peephole. My flat's like a reinforced castle.' She tried to joke about it.

'There you are then,' her neighbour said. 'Can't do more than that. Don't let these horrible people intrude any further on your life. Do you want me to ask Stanley to call in on you next week? He's coming to check on me every week at the moment; he could easily pop in.'

'That's very kind, but it won't be necessary,' Rose said. 'Thank you, though. You've given me food for thought.'

Mrs Dawson showed her out. She

smiled kindly as Rose waved goodbye. 'Take care, pet. Enjoy this lovely sunny day, and don't let the shadows in.'

Rose felt ashamed of herself. She stumbled down the last step and into the sunshine, holding her camera bag tightly. Mrs Dawson was a real trooper. She had twice the backbone that Rose had. It looked as if a gust of wind would blow her over, she was so delicate, but now Rose knew it was more likely that the wind would be blown back!

Why couldn't Rose let the incident go so easily? Truth be told, she was already suffering from broken sleep before the break-in. Ever since her dad had died, she was restless at night. She had many dreams about him, but they ended with her chasing fruitlessly after him or losing him somewhere or feeling him dissolve under her fingertips. The burglary had simply amplified her insomnia.

She walked round into the gardens at the back of the block of flats. They were well tended by the factor. Surrounded by a low green-painted fence, there were raised flower beds, a large square of mown lawn, and two benches. She let herself in and sat on a bench. Her fingers stroked the camera bag absent-mindedly.

There were plenty of photo opportunities. She could photograph the pink dahlias, golden begonias and blue delphiniums. Or take close-ups of the fat bumblebees visiting the flowers. Then of course, there were excellent zooms of the sea possible if she went out front.

Instead, she took out her camera and walked out of the gardens. She went to the shaded back of the buildings and began to click the shutter. Where could someone hide? There, at the corner of the building where the shrubbery brushed up against the brickwork. Over there, where the utility shed was. Here, under the structure of the stone staircase, where empty space lay with room enough for a crouching figure.

The phone rang just as April was about to go to her work. She rented a small warehouse in the lower end of Mayborough which she had kitted out as a kitchen and office. She and Sally baked the cakes there and decorated them. She had hired a young woman, Lucy, as her bookkeeper and office admin support. In her mind, she ran through the number of orders to be made up that day. Her business was going so well, at this rate she might have to take on more staff to fill the orders.

She was tempted not to answer the insistent shrill ringing but did so in case it was Sally calling.

'Hello?' she snapped, glancing at her wrist watch.

If it was Sally, she wanted to know why it couldn't wait the five minutes until April could get to the warehouse. But it wasn't Sally. It was her sister, Rachael.

'How are you?' Rachael asked.

April bit back a sigh. Rachael only got in contact when she needed money. 'How much do you want?' she asked.

'That's not why I'm phoning,' Rachael whined. 'I can phone my big sister, can't I?'

'How's Mum?'

'Same old, same old. She's been back to the doctor about her back but they said it's nothing. I don't trust them doctors. Her heart's been bothering her too.'

'She had all the tests and they came back clear,' April said. 'The best thing Mum can do is get out of the house and join a club. She needs to stop dwelling on everything.'

'That's easy for you to say. She's never been right after Dad left her. You're cold as ice, aren't you. Mum may have a dicky heart, but you haven't got one at all!' Rachael's voice rose shrilly.

April winced and held the receiver from her ear. She really didn't need this call right now, when she was so incredibly busy. Yet she couldn't cut Rachael's call short. Years of family obligations and guilt were ingrained in her. After their parents had gone through a particularly nasty divorce, April and Rachael had stayed with their mum while their dad took off for London. All their mum had done since, over the years, was moan about him and blame him for all her ills. Now, she and Rachael lived an hour away from Mayborough and April was glad of the distance.

'Since you mentioned money,' Rachael said, 'it wouldn't harm to have a couple of hundred to tide us over until pay day.'

'I'll write you a cheque,' April said wearily. 'There won't be more money until next month.'

'Thanks, April. You're all right.' Rachael sounded suddenly upbeat, her bad temper gone.

'I've got to go,' April said, and put the phone down.

She stared at her hands. They were

shaking badly. She clutched them together. Then she waited until gradually the shaking stopped. This couldn't go on. She was beginning to believe she had a dreadful disease. She picked up the phone and dialled the surgery. Moments later, she had a doctor's appointment for that afternoon.

She walked the short way to her part of the warehouse, not seeing the people around her. What if . . . what if she was ill? She was self-employed. That meant if she didn't work, then she didn't make any money. How would she manage? She wasn't married, she wasn't in a relationship. Her parents' marriage had put her off the idea of getting married forever. She was pleased for Goldie, of course, but she wasn't in the slightest bit envious. April liked to be in charge of her own life with no one else to please.

If only that was entirely true, she thought. She couldn't break away from her responsibilities to her mother and younger sister. She'd always felt vaguely guilty as if their parents' break-up had been due to her and Rachael. Strangely, Rachael didn't appear to share her guilt. Rachael liked nice things and spent her money without budgeting. She didn't need to. When she ran out, she phoned April, who always provided the stopgap. Rachael's job in her local supermarket didn't supply her with enough cash to give her all the pretty stuff she wanted.

April knew that her sister played on her responsibility to her family. Equally, she was unable to say to no to Rachael. She had tried. Then her mother would blame April for upsetting Rachael and for bringing on one of her 'attacks' of nerves.

'You're late today. Everything all right?' Sally smiled as April went into the kitchen.

'Perfect, thank you,' April said stiffly. 'Have you started the order?' She didn't like Sally remarking on her timing. She could be overly familiar, and April had to keep her in check. *She* was the boss and Sally was her employee. It didn't hurt to remind her of that when necessary.

'Yes, the sponges are in and I've done the red velvet cake. Do you want to see it? It's turned out marvellously.'

'Do you want me to ice it?'

Sally looked disappointed but covered it quickly with a friendly beam. 'Do you want to? I was going to put on a thick cream cheese frosting and I've got some edible violet petals for decoration.'

'No, no, you go ahead. I'll decorate the sponges from yesterday and get them sent by courier.'

April went into her office and shut the door, hiding Sally's bewildered face. Honestly, why the woman was so happy was beyond her. She'd pretend to do some paperwork before she went to her worktop. She didn't want Sally to see her hands. April held them out in front of her and watched them shiver. They weren't as bad as earlier, but there was definitely something wrong with her.

She waited for ten minutes before heading to the metal worktop and taking one of the sponge cakes to decorate. Luckily, the first order was for a simple icing-sugar frosting. Even April's hands could deal with that. Any mistakes were smoothed with a knife dipped in warm water.

Sally breezed by just as April finished. She quickly stuck her hands in her jacket pockets as her assistant stopped to admire the finished cake.

'You've such a wonderful talent for cake decorating,' Sally said. 'That icing is simply perfect. Mine is never quite so smooth. That's like glass.' She smiled.

April frowned at her. She wished Sally would move on so she could take her hands out of her pockets and get on with the next cake.

'We haven't got all day,' she snapped. 'Let's keep moving, shall we?'

She pretended not to see Sally's face drop. She turned her back as if to put a final touch to the cake. Her fingers trembled and she squeezed them into her palms, feeling the nails cut into her flesh and glad of the pain as a distraction from her fear.

★ ★ ★

'I can run some tests, but I'm fairly certain that what you're experiencing is anxiety,' the doctor said.

'Anxiety?' April said as if it was a foreign word.

'Yes. Here's a leaflet about it which gives some ideas of what you can do to relax. I want you to try them and come back and see me in three weeks' time.'

'Anxiety can make my hands shake?' She had to be sure. 'It isn't a physical disease?'

'Try the breathing exercises and the mindfulness and let's see you back.'

Mindfulness? What on earth was that? April took the leaflet and was ushered out by the doctor, whose waiting room was full. She felt a great rush of relief as his words sank in. She didn't have a terrible illness. She wasn't going to be off work. Although he had offered to sign her off. She'd told him she worked for herself. He'd warned her to keep reasonable hours and that, if her problem didn't settle, she might have to take time off.

Well, April promised herself, that wasn't going to happen. She'd do these breathing exercises and she'd do this mindfulness, whatever it was, however many times it took to get rid of her shaky hands.

She came to an abrupt stop outside her garden gate. It was open. The main door to the Victorian villa was also open. Her garden was full of packing cases, and a removals van was driving slowly off down the street.

April lived in the lower conversion of the Victorian villa. The upper conversion was empty. It had been empty the whole year she'd lived there. She'd been able to move out of her previous rented house because her business was doing so well. The estate agent had apologised for the empty floor above, but April was glad it wasn't lived in. She liked having the peace and quiet all to herself.

Except now it looked as if her peace and quiet was gone. The main door was a shared entrance. Inside there were two more doors. One led to April's home. The other, she presumed, led to a staircase to the upper level.

There was no sign of her new neighbour, so April slipped quickly into her home. With any luck, she need never see them. After all, she started work early and frequently worked late. She was only home early today because of the doctor's appointment.

She took off her jacket and hung it neatly on the coat stand in the hall, then took her handbag and set it in its usual place on the sideboard. She put her keys in the shallow raffia basket where they always lived, next to the land line telephone and her notebook for calls. Her house was neat and tidy. She breathed in the scent of lemon polish.

She went through to her kitchen. It

was a large room at the back of the house and looked out onto the rhododendrons and clipped lawn of the back garden. She had the use of the back garden while the upstairs had use of the front garden. That was what the estate agent had told her.

April loved her kitchen. It was light oak cabinets and slate marble worktops. She had an oak table and six chairs. She'd never had six visitors to sit on them, but anyway, they looked good. She very occasionally invited Goldie, Rose and Lily to dinner, and that was when her kitchen got its most use.

Generally, though, she liked to keep to herself. Her friends understood that. They invited her to their homes instead.

There was a rap at her door. April opened it to find a tall, thin man with ginger hair and a beard standing there.

'Hi, I'm your new upstairs neighbour, Steve Godley.' He held out a large hand to her.

April took it. It was warm and firm

on hers. She awkwardly took her hand back.

'April Lyons.'

'April, nice to meet you. I came down to apologise in advance in case there's any noise from the floorboards. I'm a yoga teacher, and I'll be holding a small informal class in my living room a couple of evenings a week. You're welcome to join us, if you like.'

He had an engaging grin and she felt an unwelcome flicker of interest.

'I don't think so,' she said. 'It's really not my thing. Thank you.' It came out sounding distinctly chilly, even to her ears.

His grin faded a little. He put a finger to his brow in mock salute and then disappeared through the red door to the upstairs. April stood and stared after him.

6

Goldie brought the tray of drinks over to the table. She, Rose and Lily were waiting for April at the coffee house.

'It's unlike April to be late,' Rose remarked.

'I hope she's okay,' Lily said, helping Goldie to put the drinks out. 'I haven't seen her in ages. Have you?'

'I spoke to her last night on the phone,' Goldie said, putting the tray on a nearby table, then sitting with her friends. 'She's bringing the sample wedding cakes today.'

'Is she allowed to bring cake into a coffee shop?'

Goldie laughed. 'She has a special permission from the owner today. The only condition is that we buy our drinks.'

Lily rubbed her hands together in glee. 'I can't wait. I love cake.'

April arrived, pulling what looked like a small suitcase on wheels. It was, however, a stackable set of cake tins.

'That's a great idea,' Lily said.

'It's very efficient,' April agreed. 'And it beats hauling a stack of cakes around under one's chin.'

She set the four tins out on the table while the friends all watched in anticipation.

'Okay, Goldie, I've brought you fruit cake, plain sponge, vanilla sponge and raspberry sponge to sample.'

There was a collective sigh and oohs and aahhs as April expertly flipped the lids from the cake tins to reveal what was inside.

'They smell divine,' Lily breathed.

April allowed herself a small smile. 'You'll see that they've been decorated in traditional marzipan and royal icing, and I've used Swiss buttercream filling. The piping and flowers are for demonstration purposes only. Once you've chosen your cake, I'll decorate it to your instructions and taste.'

'Oh, they're gorgeous,' Goldie cried. 'How can I choose?'

'Well, remember that your cake will be in three tiers,' April said. 'You can go for all sponge, or you can go traditional and have the bottom tier a rich fruitcake, which is why I've brought you one. Then your top tiers can be different sponge flavours. It's entirely up to you.' She paused, then added, 'Of course, if you choose to have all three tiers fruitcake, you can be even more traditional and keep the top layer for your first child's christening.'

Goldie blushed. 'Really? I've never heard of that.'

She wasn't going to tell her friends that it seemed like James didn't want children. *For a good long while*, as he put it. Her spirits dipped. They needed a conversation about that. Goldie, having brooded on his comment, had decided she definitely did want children, and soon. What was the point in waiting?

James had been in an odd mood last

night. She'd invited him over for a late supper and had made a tapas selection and opened a bottle of his favourite French red wine. She'd deliberately set up her telescope because it was to be a perfect, clear night for stargazing and she didn't want to miss it.

He appeared nervous, standing in her small living room and then following her about as she arranged the meal and took the hot food from the cooker.

'Why don't you have a seat and I'll bring the food out?' she suggested.

'I'll help you. What needs doing?'

'Nothing, really. It's all organised. I just need some space to manoeuvre. Can you step back a bit so I can see in the oven, please?'

'Sorry, darling. Shall I pour the wine?'

'Is there something wrong?' she asked eventually when he'd tripped over a tea towel and dropped a bowl on the floor, which thankfully hadn't broken. 'You're real antsy tonight.'

'Everything's as right as rain.' He took a large gulp of his wine, which he had poured despite Goldie's protest that she could manage. He glanced at her and added, 'Actually, I mentioned the drop in sales to Stella.'

'Mmm.' Goldie was only half listening. She generally tuned out when James talked about car sales as it was so deadly dull.

'You don't mind?'

'Why should I mind?'

'That I spoke to Stella about it and not you?' He was almost hopping up and down on his toes in a kind of quiet agitation.

Goldie paused with the patatas bravas on a hot tray between her oven-gloved hands. She put it down before the heat seared into her skin.

'What's this about? Did you think I'd be jealous? That I'd be upset that you spoke to your secretary?' She laughed. 'Why would I mind?'

If anything, she was glad. Stella seemed to be interested in car sales, for some unknown reason, and it meant Goldie didn't have to listen as much to it. If James could off-load to Stella, so much the better, she reasoned.

So why was James going a beetroot red? Goldie slowly slid the oven gloves off and laid them beside the patatas bravas.

'James?'

'It was nothing,' he blustered. Clumsily he poured more wine, and Goldie watched it splash on the glass's rim and dribble onto the kitchen worktop. She mopped it up as her mind whirled. What was going on? Had James cheated on her with Stella? It sounded preposterous.

'What was nothing?' Her voice was frosty.

'Only, she was standing rather close as we spoke. That's all. I . . . ' He trailed away.

Suddenly, Goldie didn't want to know. Their wedding was less than a month, away and she'd worked so hard to make sure it was her Goldilocks wedding. She wasn't going to allow it to be derailed now.

'Let's go and eat,' she said, taking his hand and drawing him into the living room.

Their meal was nice, the tapas tasty and the wine of good vintage. Goldie made small talk to cover the awkwardness that hung around her fiancé like a fog. She deliberately didn't mention his work and neither did he. When she suggested they stargaze, for once he didn't grumble or decline. Instead, he was enthusiastic as if he wanted to make it up to her. For what, Goldie didn't care to ask. They were back on track, that was what mattered. She wasn't going to muse about Stella. She wasn't important, but Goldie and James were.

Now, she took the slices of cake that April offered her and took a bite of the fruitcake.

'That is truly delicious,' she said.

Beside her, Lily and Rose were giggling as they sampled the cakes and sipped their coffees. April went to the counter to order more drinks. Goldie felt a shot of excitement rise up. It was really happening. In another few weeks, she'd be Mrs Goldie Smith. She looked at her beautiful engagement ring, sparkling in the sunlight. Life was wonderful. She was very happy. If a tiny worm of discomfort wriggled in her stomach when she thought of James, then she ignored it.

'Oh, I must show you these,' Lily cried, rummaging in her over-large cotton bag. She came out with a small bundle of photographs and handed them to Rose.

'They're soooo cute. Whose are they?'

Goldie peered over Rose's shoulder to see what the fuss was about. The photos showed two tiny black kittens. Rose was right; they were incredibly cute.

'Let me guess.' Goldie grinned. 'They're Lily's kittens.'

'Top marks,' Lily said. 'Someone

dumped them on my doorstep yesterday, so I guess they're mine now.'

'How many cats do you have?' April asked, returning with the drinks, her mouth twisted in disgust. 'I hate cats. They smell.'

'Is that why you rarely visit me?' Lily joked.

'You don't want to get a reputation as a mad cat lady, that's all I'm saying,' April said.

'She has a reputation as a lady who cares,' Rose said loyally. She handed the photos back to Lily. 'Those are lucky little kittens to find you.'

April tidied the cake doilies and ignored Rose.

'How's the organising of the hen party coming along?' Goldie asked hastily.

'I forgot I was going to tell you about it,' Lily said. 'It's not long now, and I wanted to say to you to wear sensible shoes.'

Goldie's eyebrows rose. 'Sensible shoes? Where on earth are we going?'

Lily shook her head. 'I can't tell you, but Rose and April know all the gory details.'

'I hate that I'm out of a secret between you guys,' Goldie complained with a smile.

'That's your fault for getting married and leaving us all on the shelf,' Lily quipped.

She turned to share the joke with Rose and saw her friend's eyes flicker.

'What? You've met someone, haven't you?'

'No. Or . . . maybe.'

'How could you? We were just talking the other day about how very single we are and how there are no decent men in Mayborough!'

Now three pairs of eyes bored into Rose. She squirmed a little on her seat and took a nibble of sponge cake to fortify herself. Clearly, she wasn't going to get away with silence.

'You all know how my flat got broken into,' she began, and three heads nodded.

107

She hadn't told them about her nightmares and terror and she wasn't going to now.

'I had a visitor yesterday. A community policeman called Ben.'

* * *

Rose had been at home and at her drawing board. The illustrations for Dorey Stephen's book were coming on well. She was using fine coloured inks to bring out the woodland creatures. She had ideas for shading the backgrounds and for how the final picture would look. The doorbell ringing took her by surprise. She laid down her pen and went to the peephole.

She didn't recognise the man standing outside, and hesitated. But it was mid-afternoon and daylight. Also, he was wearing a fluorescent jacket and what looked like a policeman's uniform.

She opened the door. A tall, broad-shouldered young man stood there. He had sandy hair and big brown eyes. When she looked into them, they were like a pool of warmth and compassion. It didn't hurt that he was very good-looking. She became aware that she was staring and hadn't said a word. But equally odd, he was staring at her too, as if they were the only living beings in the entire world.

Before things could get really weird, Rose gave a small cough. 'Hi, can I help you?'

'Rose Redd?' His voice was deliciously low and made her think of thick caramel.

She nodded.

'I'm Ben Scott, the community policeman. Can I come in for a moment?'

She stepped back and he followed her in. She sat on her sofa and he sat opposite, his long legs bumping the low table. There was another silence, not unpleasant but slightly unreal. Rose couldn't stop drinking him in. He was gorgeous. Afraid she was being rude, she tried to start a conversation.

'What can I do for you?'

At the same moment, he spoke. 'Rose Redd? Isn't that a fairy tale character?'

Rose smiled. 'My Mum loves fairy tales. With the gift of a surname like Redd, she couldn't resist naming me after Snow White and Rose Red. It's not one of the better known fairy tales but it's her favourite.'

'I like it. That's neat.'

She liked him. She wondered if the surge of electricity she felt sitting opposite him was visible. Was she giving off sparks? She felt as if she was lit up from inside, like the Christmas tree in Mayborough town square every year with its baubles and string of lights.

'So, I'm here because you had a break-in,' Ben said, taking out a notebook. 'In fact, you weren't the only one in the building to suffer, so we're going to have a police presence over the next few weeks. There's been a spate of burglaries in the neighbourhood and we're concerned about that.'

Rose was glad to hear it. Perhaps knowing there were more police about would help her get to sleep easier. Especially if it was Ben on patrol. She answered his questions. She'd given all this information to the other police officer, so knew it all off by heart. That gave her time to concentrate on him. How when he smiled, a dimple appeared in his left cheek just by his mouth. How his mouth was full for a man, no thin lips in sight. His hair had a kink in it and the hint of curls cropped short.

After a while, he stopped talking. Rose hoped she'd spoken sensibly. She hadn't paid much attention.

'I'm off duty at six o'clock,' Ben said. 'Would you like to have a drink with me?'

'Yes please,' Rose said, and then felt foolish. *Yes please*. What kind of idiot was she? She couldn't think straight when he stared at her like that. Inside, she was quivering, but it felt good. Like a cloud of butterflies in rainbow colours dancing.

'And so we had a drink together,' she finished her story to her gaping friends.

'Don't stop there,' Lily cried. 'What's he like? What did you talk about? Has he got any good-looking friends?'

'Are you certain he's single?' April frowned. 'He sounds a bit slick, interviewing you for a serious crime and asking you out for a drink in the same breath. Maybe he does that with all the pretty women he meets in his work.'

'It's very romantic, Rose, so ignore April's grumps,' Goldie said. 'Who knows, you might be the next one getting married.'

Rose put up her hands to stem the excited chatter. 'Whoa, hold your horses, guys. It was one drink.' Then she sighed. 'No, it wasn't simply one drink. I'm in love with Ben. It was love at first sight. He feels the same for me.'

'He told you he loves you?' Goldie was astonished. It had taken James four years to propose to her and to tell her he loved her.

'Not in so many words, but . . . I *know*. Just as I know he's the one for me. He's the man I'm going to spend the rest of my life with.'

'Did you talk at all?' Lily asked. 'Or did you gaze into each other's eyes all night?'

'We talked. Ben's a keen footballer; he plays for the Mayborough town team. He also plays golf and likes to go fishing. In fact, I'm going to watch his next match at the weekend.'

'But you hate sport.'

Rose shrugged and threw her friends a big dopey smile. 'I don't care. I'd watch Ben do cartwheels or dance the tango. As long as I can be with him.'

'You've got a bad dose of it,' April remarked sourly.

'You must invite him to the wedding,' Goldie said. 'You've all got invitations for you plus one, so make Ben your plus one.'

'Great idea. I will, thanks Goldie.'

Lily sighed. 'I wish I had a plus one to invite.'

'What about your cousin, Neville?'

'Thanks, Neville's a lovely cousin but I'm not taking him as my partner to your wedding. I'd rather come alone. Are you bringing anyone, April?'

April looked shocked. 'No, of course not.'

'Why is it 'of course not'? You sound like I just asked you to boil your head.'

'I'm not going out with anyone, as you know fine well, and I've no intention of doing so either.'

'You surely don't want to be on your own forever?'

'I like my own company. I have no desire to be at someone else's beck and call.'

April began to take the remains of the cakes and slide them back into the cake tins.

'Let me know when you've made your mind up about the cake tiers. And don't forget to give me some ideas for decorations, if you want it personalised.

I've got to go. See you all soon.'

They all left soon after April's abrupt departure. Rose felt like she was dancing along on fluffy clouds as she wandered home. Ben, Ben, Ben. She rolled his name around on her lips. She was still happy later that evening as she got into her pyjamas and brushed her teeth. She leapt into bed and turned on her bedside lamp. She got her book and propped up her pillow.

She woke up with a start. The room was dark. Confused, she fumbled for the switch for her bedroom lamp. It didn't work. She kept pressing it but the bulb refused to go on. Her heart began to pound. Then she heard a noise. A creaking sound as if someone was in her living room, treading carefully on the floor.

Now her heart was hammering in her chest. The hairs on the back of neck stood up. She tried to think of Ben. But it didn't help. Instead of calming her, she thought why did they send a community policeman? Resources were tight, weren't they? It stood to reason they sent Ben because they were sure another burglary was likely.

It was here! Right here! In her flat. Someone was creeping towards her bedroom door. She pulled her lamp free from the wall. It was her only weapon. Wait. They'd expect her to be in her bed.

She slid as silently as possible from her bed, her lamp gripped in her palm. Her forehead was damp with sweat. Her chest was painful. Her ribs were bruised from tension. She stared at the door. Was it going to open? Was an intruder going to burst in?

Minutes passed. Then more minutes. Rose held her breath but had to let it go. Finally, when there was no action, she made it to the wall and switched on the bedroom light. She pushed her bedroom door open.

Her living room was as it always was. There was her sofa, her low coffee table, the two easy chairs. The gaping space where her television should have been. No intruder. No broken door bashed in.

She put on the living room light anyway. Then she sat on the sofa and sobbed. Finally she got dressed and packed her small suitcase. She took the telephone and dialled.

'Mayborough Hotel? Yes, I'd like to book a room for tonight, please. Can you send a taxi to pick me up?'

7

'I'd forgotten how quaint this place is.'

Lisa Rayner strode along the seafront at Mayborough as though she was in a military parade. Goldie struggled to keep up; her strappy sandals with their slim high heels were not ideal for a morning jog.

'Yeah, honey, it sure is.' Dirk Rayner, Goldie's father, looked about with barely concealed amusement.

If they were finding her home town humorous, they were gaining some strange looks themselves, Goldie thought in horror. They stood out, with their military bearing and short haircuts. They weren't in uniform, but might as well have had US Army emblazoned on their foreheads.

Dirk's buzz cut hair was dark with grey temples. Goldie noted the grey hair with a pang. When had that happened? He was tanned and well-muscled and lean, and she noticed that people stepped out of his way. Lisa was equally sun-kissed, making her turquoise eyes appear sharp. Goldie's Mom missed nothing. She was the cleverest woman Goldie knew. She'd always felt daunted and dumb next to her mother.

'So, what's the plan?' Dirk asked.

He was a man of action and got twitchy if asked to sit for long periods.

'I was a little thrown at you arriving early,' Goldie said, thankful they'd stopped to stare out at the sea for a moment so she could catch her breath. 'I thought you were coming a week before the wedding, not ten days before.'

'Our leave got changed last minute,' Lisa told her. 'We took off as soon as we packed. No point in hanging around, especially as we have to go back Stateside straight after the wedding.'

'You came from America, not South

Korea?' Goldie wasn't sure where to start with what Lisa had said. She was deeply disappointed that they were leaving right after the wedding. She'd planned to show them about and spend some quality time with them before she and James went on honeymoon a week after they got married.

'Yeah, we're based in Washington since a few months ago.'

'You never told me.'

'Didn't we? Does it matter? You know you can call on the cell phone any time, right?'

'I know that, but I like to know where you are, that's all.'

'We're right here, honey, that's where we are.' Dirk put his arm around Goldie's shoulder and shook her in a comradely manner.

'Thanks, Dad,' she said weakly. 'I'd kind of hoped you guys would be about after the wedding so we could catch up a bit.'

'No can do, kiddo. We've got our orders.' Lisa didn't look too upset, her keen gaze flickering over the holiday-makers on the beach as if searching for trouble.

Goldie wished, not for the first time, that she had normal parents. Lisa and Dirk looked as if they were ready to take down the bad men at the first sign of gunfire. Which was hardly likely in sleepy Mayborough.

Dirk clapped his hands smartly. 'So, what's the plan?'

'I thought we'd walk along the promenade, and then we're due at James's parents' house for lunch. I wish you'd let me know when you were arriving, then I could've picked you up at the airport.'

'No need for us to put you out,' Lisa said. 'We can book in at this Mansion House Hotel this afternoon, can we?'

'That's where we're going for lunch,' Goldie explained. 'James's parents own it and that's where the wedding reception will be. We're getting married in Mayborough Church. I can show you it, if you like. You might remember it from when we all lived here.'

There was no sign of interest from either parent. They started walking along the promenade again and Goldie hurried to catch up. Dirk's arm slid around his wife's waist and Goldie felt the same, childish emotion from years ago. She was the odd one out. They didn't need her. They had never needed her. They were, in themselves, complete.

Goldie guided them along the promenade and back via the lovely old stone church anyway. She wanted them to be involved in this. She was making memories for all of them. Surely at some point in the future, her parents would retire from the army, and then there'd be time to reminisce about all the good old days. Her wedding would be right up there with the best of them.

'I can send you photos of the big day,' she said eagerly as she pointed out exactly where she and James would stand for the photographs. 'Or did you bring a camera?'

'We've got our cell phones.'

'I don't think the quality will be good enough. I'll send you some of the formal shots.'

Goldie smiled as she looked at the church entrance. In only ten short days, she'd be standing there in her beautiful wedding dress, with her antique veil and bouquet of flowers. James would look wonderful in his embroidered waistcoat and top hat and silk cravat. She sighed with pleasure. She shouldn't worry so much. It was all going to go fine.

'Great. You do that, honey.' Dirk paced the inside perimeter of the tiny church yard. It was a low, ancient stone wall clad in lichens and small purple flowers.

Lisa glanced at her wrist watch. 'Eleven hundred hours. We got time for this? We oughta get our stuff to the hotel. Dirk, let's go.'

'Wait. Please. There's no hurry.' Goldie wanted to hold off on lunch as long as she could.

But a few minutes later, she couldn't take the tension. Her parents weren't interested in the old church. They were standing there to be polite. Goldie didn't want polite. She wanted . . . she wanted parents who cared. She'd forgotten just how wrapped up in their own affairs they were. It made her all the more determined to put down good, solid roots by marrying James.

She vowed that when she had children, she'd always be there for them. She'd read them bedtime stories and listen to their chatter. She'd never leave them on one continent to pursue a career across an ocean.

Whatever differences she had with James, they'd make it work.

* * *

Lily wasn't one of life's great worriers. But even she was feeling a little anxious as she sat in her garden looking at her notebook. She kept a loose note of her budget there, her incomings and outgoings. There were gaps and cross outs and asterisks where she'd forgotten to put in some figures, but basically it was all there. And it wasn't looking the best.

She shut the notebook for a moment and sucked in the sweet, fresh air. She was a great believer in mindfulness. It was the art of staying in the present moment, not regretting the past or fearing the future. She focussed right in on the sound of birdsong and the whispering of the leaves above her.

She had a lot to be thankful for. She rented a really lovely place to live out here in nature. She was the proud owner of a campervan. She had a job she liked. Okay, it didn't pay that well, but she loved talking to the school pupils as she drove them here and there.

She loved her animals too. Which was why she wished they weren't the problem. She was used to people giving her sick birds or hedgehogs to care for. She'd been given Humphrey by an old lady in town who could no longer look after him. The ginger tom and the black and white cat were strays who'd found their own way to her. Rowena had been a gift from nature. Soon, Lily could release her back into the wild. It was the kittens that were the problem.

She'd been excited at the arrival of the first two kittens. Someone had left them on her doorstep in a cardboard box. Lily had found them when she returned from work. They were curled up together on top of a thick wad of newspaper. Whoever had left them had cared enough to make sure they were comfortable. She was a little concerned that no food or drink had accompanied them. After all, the person wasn't to know that Lily would be coming home that day. What if she'd been away for a few days? It didn't bear thinking about.

She'd gladly taken them in and fed them. She enjoyed watching them cavort around her room. No small creature was as playful as a kitten. They made her laugh. She wasn't laughing quite so much when this morning she'd found another box on her doorstep.

This time, there were four kittens. Three tabbies and a black one. Lily guessed they were from the same litter as the other two. Why had she been brought them in two visits? More importantly, who was bringing them?

She hadn't heard a car drawing up, or the crunch of footsteps on gravel or even on the creaky front wooden step of her cabin. The donator of kittens was sneaky. She'd give them that. There were no clues.

She took up her jotter again. But however many times she looked at the page, she couldn't make the figures change for the better. Cat food was expensive. Lily's wages were low. She'd already been just about balancing the books before all the kittens arrived. Never mind kitten food, what about kitten health checks and kitten vaccinations?

She picked one of her tiny problems

up and stroked it. The kitten purred loudly.

'I might have to give you away, little one,' she said sadly. 'I don't want to. I like to have my animal sanctuary right here under my wooden roof, but it can't go on. I can't save you all.' She kissed its soft furry head and gently put it down on the ground. The kitten wobbled, then bounced off to play with its brother's tail.

'Maybe Rose can advise me what to do,' she mused out loud. 'Hey, maybe Rose would like a kitten or three to keep her company in her flat. I hope Ben isn't allergic to cats.'

She rang Rose's landline and waited. It rang and rang. With a shrug, Lily put the phone down. She'd tried the day before too, and Rose wasn't answering. She wasn't picking up her mobile either. If Lily didn't hear from her soon, she was going to drive into town and make sure Rose was okay.

She thought about phoning Goldie or April. Then she remembered April's comments on cats. She hated cats. Goldie, then. Lily's fingers hovered over the mobile's buttons. It wasn't fair to ask Goldie what to do. All she could talk about was weddings and more wedding stuff. Lily was sick of hearing about nuptials. Only she mustn't show it. Goldie was so happy. And Lily was happy for her. Even if she had her doubts about her friend marrying her brother.

She sat in her garden and played with the kittens. Perhaps a solution would come to her. Right now, it didn't seem likely. Something had to happen. Lily jumped up, startling her small play mates. She'd track down the person.

Where was the cardboard box? Maybe there were clues. Lily rushed inside to get it.

★   ★   ★

Goldie walked aimlessly around town. Lunch had been a disaster. Her parents were very different from Hugh and Margery and unfortunately, it showed. They had different views on everything, and Goldie and James had desperately searched for neutral topics to keep the conversation going. Margery had arrived late for lunch, flustered. Lisa and Dirk had frowned at this. Punctuality was key. That was a phrase drummed into Goldie from an early age. Therefore, lunch started badly, then went downhill.

Hugh asked if they like hunting and proceeded to go into length about his latest hunting trip. He seemed oblivious to Lisa and Dirk's distaste. James tried to help by deflecting the conversation to car sales. Hugh brought it swiftly back. He hadn't finished describing shooting squirrels. Since neither hunting nor cars were of interest to Goldie's parents, it didn't matter.

Finally, everyone concentrated on their food and conversation halted. Goldie was relieved when lunch finished up and she was free to go. She'd hoped James might have time to go with her for a coffee, but he hurried back to work. Thus, here she was. She had taken annual leave while her parents were here. She had no work to scurry off to.

She looked up to find herself outside the Laidlaws' house. Bryce's mum had looked after her in the years she'd rented a room from them. While Bryce had gone to university, Goldie had attended the local college and then quickly found an office job in Mayborough. Morag Laidlaw had been like a second mother. She'd moved south after her husband died and took in lodgers to make ends meet. But Goldie always felt more than a lodger. Morag made her feel special.

She pushed open the garden gate and went in. There was a whistling from round the side and sounds of twigs snapping. Curious, she stepped round. Bryce was attacking a large shrub with a pair of loppers.

'Hey.'

He stopped and grinned, wiping his

forehead with the back of his wrist. 'Hey, yourself. What brings you here?'

'I'm the shrub protection officer. I got a call saying you were beating up an azalea.'

'Wrong house then. This isn't an azalea, it's a buddleia, and my mother wants it brought down to size.'

'Very well, I won't arrest you this time. Seriously, are you sure you're meant to be pruning in the middle of summer? I'm fairly certain pruning is an autumn task.'

'You're an expert in gardening? I never knew,' Bryce teased as he laid down the loppers and stepped back to survey his handiwork.

'That's not fair,' Goldie pouted. 'I have a very nice garden.'

'Only because Lily comes and tends it for you.'

She laughed. 'Okay, you win. Is your mum home? I'd love to see her.'

'And here I thought you'd come to visit me.'

'You should be so lucky.'

If they weren't careful, this was almost like flirting, she caught herself thinking. No, it was banter. This was Bryce, after all. A man who didn't like to take things seriously. Which was partly why they'd broken up all those years ago at high school. Goldie had wanted more than just fun. Bryce hadn't.

It was a pity they hadn't met later in life, she mused. They'd lit a candle together that burned brightly but went out equally fast. There was no sign Bryce had changed. As far as she knew, he didn't have a long-term girlfriend. Although she saw him with enough female friends to know he didn't lack company.

'I'll go and find Morag.' She smiled and left him getting ready to tackle the lower branches of the buddleia.

'Goldie, it's wonderful to see you.' Morag Laidlaw's Scottish accent hadn't softened in her years in the town. It had a lilt that reminded Goldie of a melody. 'Come on in and have some lemonade.

133

I made it this morning for Bryce. Did you see him? He's tidying up the garden for me. I've got new lodgers arriving. I'm letting out three rooms now, I feel it's almost a bed and breakfast hotel!'

'Whoever they are, they're very lucky to be boarding with you. If my experience is to go by, they'll be pampered terribly and won't want to leave.'

'You needed pampering,' Morag told her. 'I can't imagine what it was like being eighteen and no parents around to help and support you.'

'Talking of parents, Lisa and Dirk have arrived for the wedding. I've just left them getting settled in at the Mansion House Hotel.'

'I'm so glad they came for your big day. I did wonder if they'd manage to get away. They're so busy all over the world.'

Goldie laughed. 'You're being very tactful. But I love you for it.'

She took the glass of lemonade that

Morag offered and they sat in the cheerful kitchen which looked out on a neat lawn and colourful flower beds. There was a companionable silence for a while but Goldie was aware of Morag's keen eyes assessing her.

'What is it?' she said. 'I can tell you've got something on your mind. Want to spit it out?'

Morag's expression was serious. 'You can stop this at any time, you know that? You don't have to go through with it. You must be certain, absolutely sure that James is the one for you.'

'Have you been chatting to Lily?' Goldie joked feebly.

Morag reached out and stroked her hand. 'I love you as if I were your mother, Goldie. I looked after you for four years while you became the lovely, confident woman you are today. I helped you when you struggled with your exam revision and when you broke up with Bryce. I know you and I want you to be ever so happy in life.'

Goldie pulled her hand away. 'You do

135

know me, but no one but me knows what's in my heart. I love James and that's who I'm going to marry. If you hoped that Bryce and I . . . that we'd somehow make up, and grow up, and get together, then I'm sorry, that's not going to happen.'

She stood up abruptly, tears threatening. She had enough pre-wedding nerves and uncertainty without the people she cared about making her doubt further. She walked out of the kitchen, bumping into Bryce as he came through. She didn't stop to apologise. Her vision blurred as she hurried out onto the street, going where she didn't know.

8

Goldie wore jean shorts and a pink T-shirt. She slid on her trainers over white sport socks and tied her hair back in a ponytail. Makeup or naked face? She wrinkled her nose at her mirror reflection. Naked. She splashed some sunscreen onto her palm and rubbed it in to her skin. A light dusting of face powder and she was ready. The question was, ready for what?

Bryce's text had been short and to the point. *Taking you on an outing. Sporty. Bring sandwich.* It was another dry day, a little overcast but with the promise of sunshine later. She was now looking sporty. She also had a sandwich. Or rather two ham and salad sandwiches, a bottle of orange juice and two blackberry muffins, courtesy of the local corner shop. She put the lunch into a cotton bag and added a jacket, just in case.

The sound of a car engine made her run to the window. She clapped her hand to her mouth. What on earth? Bryce waved to her to get down and tapped exaggeratedly at his watch. She waved back. Her thoughts, however, were on the two kayaks fixed to his car roof. Sporty. His text said it all.

She clattered downstairs and out to meet him. Bryce unwound his long body and stretched.

'What are those?' Goldie asked ominously, pointing up at the roof rack.

'I'm going to let you have three guesses.' He yawned and then took her bag for her. 'It's way too early. I must be mad letting you talk me into this.'

'Me?' she squeaked. 'I was fast asleep when your text blasted my eardrum. It's Saturday, for goodness sake. I'm meant to be having a lie-in.'

'Shouldn't have your mobile so close to your head when you're sleeping. It's terribly bad for you.'

'Getting up at seven a.m. is bad for

me. Maybe I'll just head straight back to bed.' She half turned before he grabbed her arm.

'Hey, come on. We're going to have fun.'

'Why do we have to have fun?' she grumbled as they got into the car.

'Because my mother told me we have to.'

'Morag told you to take me out today?'

Bryce manoeuvred out past the other parked cars, and the warm summer air drifted in through the open windows. It smelt of rich soil, perfumed petals and sea salt. Goldie heard the happy screams of children down on the beach and the call of the gulls overhead. A low folk song wafted from the car radio and she turned it down. She wanted to hear what Morag had to do with the surprise outing.

'My mother's concerned that you're stressed. She wants you to have a day playing hooky from weddings. You're not even to think about getting married. That's her orders by the way, not mine. It's okay by me if you want to think about it. Oh, and she says she's sorry for making you cry.'

'It wasn't her fault. I'm a bit weepy these days anyway. It's very sweet of her to organise this.'

'She *ordered* it, she didn't *organise* it.' Bryce risked a glance over at her before focussing on the road ahead, 'Yours truly did the organising. Very last minute. Did you know you can hire kayaks from Mr Gibson at the garage? I didn't until I googled local kayak hire.'

'Yes, the kayaks . . . '

'Come on, Goldie, you remember how to kayak, don't ya? We spent ages kayaking at high school. I seem to recall you were on the kayak team.'

'The words 'high school' say it all. That was ten, long years ago. I haven't kayaked since. Have you?'

There was a pause.

'How hard can it be?' came the jaunty reply.

Goldie rolled her eyes.

They parked at a bay parking plot overlooking the lake. There was a backdrop of low hills, and the land around the lake was splashed with yellow and purple of gorse and willow herb blooms.

'This is pretty,' Goldie breathed.

'Hasn't changed much, has it? I haven't been here in years. Probably since those long-ago days.'

'Come off it, you have so been here. What about whatshername? Susan, that's it. She loved nature, and was always dragging you out here hiking round the lake.'

'To paraphrase you, that was long years ago. I wonder what Susan's up to now. Probably married that bank trainee she dumped me for. She'll be rolling in money now and thankful for the choices she made.'

'Susan dumped you?' Goldie raised her eyebrows in mock horror. 'I assumed you inevitably did the dumping.'

Bryce threw her a wry smile. 'You

have a short memory.'

'What?'

'After all, you dumped me at the end of high school. So don't blame poor old Susan for doing the dastardly deed when you did it too.'

'Are you trying for the sympathy vote? Cos it ain't working.'

Goldie kept her tone light and teasing. She didn't want to think about how painful it had been breaking up with Bryce. Even if it was ten years ago, it still hurt. She had wanted a meaningful relationship with a future. Bryce, it seemed, wanted a girlfriend with no strings attached.

'Did you bring life jackets?' she asked, changing the subject.

They paddled away from shore, across the clear green water. Tiny shoals of fish darted away beneath Goldie's kayak. Ahead of them was the island, clothed in pine trees and granite rocks. It wasn't far, but she felt the pull of her muscles as she paddled. She was out of condition. How long was it since she'd taken some exercise? Too long. All her hours were absorbed by either work or wedding.

With a shock, she realised Morag was right — she did need a break. A day of simple fun. She was touched that Bryce's mum had thought of this. She always had known what Goldie needed. But not when it came to James. Morag was wrong. Goldie did want to marry James. She was determined to. In fact, she wished James was here now. Never mind that he hated sports. They had that in common. They spent their time together shopping or eating out. He couldn't kayak. Still, she promised herself to organise a meal with him the next evening he had free. He was so busy lately.

'Isn't this marvellous?' Bryce shouted over to her.

She looked at him. He was paddling with ease, keeping pace with her. He looked totally in his element, his dark hair flicked back with the breeze and his face tanned. His arm muscles flexed as he wielded the paddle.

'It's great,' she said sincerely.

She glided along, enjoying the warm day and the peace and quiet.

'Last one to the island makes the lunch,' Bryce called.

Before she could respond, he was off, paddle flashing and wavelets frothing in his wake.

'Wait!'

She began to paddle furiously. Her kayak sped up and she felt her heart pumping madly. Bryce was ahead, going well. She put all her strength into it. She was closing the gap. She was almost there. She could reach out and touch him. The beach ground under his kayak and he whooped in triumph. Goldie's kayak slid neatly onto the sand, and Bryce reached out and pulled it in.

'I hope you like making lunch.' He grinned.

'Ha! If you were any kind of gentleman, you'd have let me win.'

'Let you win? Are you crazy? What

kind of idiot would that make me? I'm not the kind to let you win. You have to make it real.' He shook his head in disgust. 'Oh, and Goldie?'

'Yes, Bryce?'

'Don't forget the bag with lunch in it, will you?'

She threw the bag at him but he caught it with a wide grin. She found herself grinning back. All her cares vanished. They tramped through the pine needle carpet to the far side of the island. They were totally alone. Through the trees, she glimpsed the water and a few pleasure craft drifting along.

'This is the best place for a picnic,' Bryce said, throwing his day sack down.

'Totally.' Goldie slid down onto the sand beside him.

They were on the unspoilt beach at the wilder side of the island. This part looked out over the smooth expanse of lake water to the mainland beyond which was mostly farm fields and dotted farm houses. The valley with

Mayborough was behind them, hidden by the island trees. It felt very peaceful and isolated.

'What is for lunch?' Bryce asked, resting his folded arms behind his head and closing his eyes.

'Sandwiches, which is what you asked me to bring. Isn't it a little early for lunch?'

But when she checked, it was midday already. The drive out to the lake had taken longer than she expected. Plus, the kayaking wasn't fast. She took out the sandwiches, the muffins and the drinks.

'Playing hooky is fun,' she said. 'We should do this more often.'

He squinted an eye at her. Goldie looked away quickly. What a fool she was. They wouldn't be doing this often or possibly ever again, once she was married. She knew James wouldn't approve and she didn't blame him. She could hardly marry one man and have days out with another.

That realisation made her suddenly

sad. Was this it? Was she never to enjoy Bryce's company again once she and James had tied the knot?

'Where are your parents today? I forgot about them. I hope I haven't dragged you away from a day out with them?' Bryce pushed himself up on one elbow and gazed at her.

Goldie shook her head. 'They decided to go into the city today. Dad needs a cravat for the wedding.'

'That's a forbidden word today, according to Mum.'

'Sorry. No, Mom and Dad are busy, so we don't need to worry about them. James is working. April called me to say the cake is ready. Okay, okay, that's a bit wedding-ey, so I won't mention the cake, *The Cake*, again. Except to say it sounds utterly delicious. Lily was driving some rich kid from the boarding school to the airport for a flight to Dubai. And as for Rose, well I haven't the faintest. I keep calling her but getting no answer. Have you seen her lately?'

'Last I saw her, I bumped into her by accident the other day. She was as skittish as a cat, nearly jumped out of her skin until she saw it was me. She was taking photos; no surprise there, but she didn't chat much. I got the impression I was in the way, so I left her.'

'Her flat got broken into, which was horrible, but she met the community policeman and fell in love with him so I guess it ended happily enough,' Goldie murmured, closing her own eyes for just a moment.

The sun was hot on her eyelids. She felt a tickle as if an insect had landed on her. She brushed it off and sat up. Had she fallen asleep? Bryce was no longer by her side. He was down at the water's edge. Sleepily, she stood up and went down to join him. He was skimming pebbles.

'Feeling refreshed?'

'Did I sleep for long?' She pushed her long hair back from her face.

'About an hour.'

'You're kidding.'

'Nope. I'm starving.' He skimmed a pebble that bounced for ten.

'I should be pleased you waited for me. And glad you didn't eat it all.' She flicked a pebble in and watched it sink, surrounded by rippling circles of glassy green. 'Want to eat now? Let me get the stuff.'

They sat at the water's edge. Goldie took off her trainers and let water lap at her toes.

'Are you bringing a plus one to the wedding?' she asked.

Bryce munched his sandwich and waved a finger at her.

'I know, I know, Morag's rules. But she's not here, and I want an answer. Is there a new Susan in your life?'

Why was she torturing herself like this? It was almost as if, knowing their time together was running out like the tide, she wanted to needle and inflict pain. It was like sticking a knife into her stomach and twisting it.

Bryce licked his fingers, reached for a

muffin. Goldie watched his movements, almost holding her breath.

'I'll be coming alone.'

'Oh.'

'What is it, Goldie? Is it not enough that you and James are getting hitched — but you want everyone else to neatly tie up in twos as well?'

'Don't be so harsh with me. I just want you to be happy, that's all.'

'I am happy.'

'Happy being alone? Do you think you'll ever meet the right woman and want to settle down?'

'Goldie,' he warned. He scrunched up the muffin wrapper and threw it into the bag.

'What?' she said. 'I'm not allowed to want one of my oldest and best friends to meet someone special?'

'Goldie,' he said again but his tone was softer, deeper, and suddenly warning bells were sounding.

'After all, they say there's someone for everyone somewhere in the world. Not for April, because she doesn't want to; she wants to be on her own,' Goldie wished she could stop speaking but it was gushing out.

'What if I *am* ready to settle down, but the girl I want is already spoken for?' Bryce said quietly.

Now the opposite occurred. Goldie's words dried up in her mouth. She stared out at the water numbly. Bryce was hunched over his long legs.

She turned to him. 'I'm sorry. I had no idea.'

'No idea? Are you being naive or disingenuous? You've always known how I feel about you. If you hadn't broken it off in college — '

'We were too young, you've said it yourself. You weren't serious about me back then. You wanted a pretty girl on your arm, a girlfriend to take to parties, that was all. I wanted us to mean something. I wanted us to be headed somewhere. Together. That's why I broke up with you. Because I saw it wasn't going to happen.'

Their eyes were locked. Goldie's

chest heaved up and down. Bryce's jaw was tight and a small muscle flickered there. She was the first to look away.

'It doesn't matter now. It's too late. It's all away back in the past.' Her lips were numb.

'You're right. It doesn't matter. Come on, I'll take you home.'

At that moment, the first raindrops fell. They were icy cold on her scalp. They rustled like music on the plastic lunch bag. The smooth glass of the lake was now pitted and the sky was grey. Goldie stumbled to her feet. Bryce grabbed his day sack and the bag and they ran for the shelter of the trees.

Kayaking back was a chore. The rain fell even heavier. It trickled coldly down the back of her neck and soaked her shorts and T-shirt. A cool, stiff breeze started up. It ruffled the water and chilled her. She looked at Bryce. He was ahead of her, arms moving fast and rhythmically. He didn't look back.

She'd angered him. His ramrod back

was proof of that. Why had she kept on at him? Goldie mentally kicked herself. What had she wanted? She didn't know. All she knew was she was very confused. And that she was in danger of losing him. That mattered. It mattered a great deal.

He didn't speak to her as he hauled the kayaks out onto the shore. He refused her help as he lifted them and lashed them to the car roof. Goldie sat shivering in the passenger seat, feeling useless. Finally, he got into the car and slammed the driver door. They sat there and the windows misted up.

With a sound of annoyance, Bryce switched on the engine and the air flow. Gradually, heat filled the small space and the front window de-misted. All the while, Goldie sat, unsure what to say to make things better.

He was so close, she felt his body heat. His scent was of damp male skin, pine resin and something that was simply Bryce. She wished they could go back to before today. To the easy companionship she thought they'd shared.

'Are we still friends?' she whispered.

His fingers paused on the ignition key. Then he turned it and revved the car.

'I'll always be your friend, Goldie.'

He dropped her back home and sped away without waving. Goldie wondered if it was true. Would he always be her friend? Because right now, it felt like they weren't friends at all. She thought how pleased James would be if she told him she and Bryce had fallen out. He didn't like Bryce. Had he seen him as a threat? Maybe James was the only one seeing things clearly.

Goldie ran herself a hot bubbly bath. It was summer, but she was chilled right down to the bone. When it was full, she sank into it up to her neck. What a mess it all was. She felt tears slide down her cheeks and rubbed them away with the hot soapy water. She had no idea how to make things right.

She lay there, her mind whirling. What was Morag going to say when Bryce told her what a disaster their day had been? Goldie was upsetting everyone. That was how it felt. Morag and Bryce. James too was off-key with his remarks about Stella and his strange behaviour the other evening. Rose wasn't answering her calls. Had Goldie somehow irritated her too? April hadn't made contact except about the cake. Lily had snapped at her when she'd mentioned Davey's bouquets over the phone.

Goldie sat in her cooling bath and cried.

9

'You want to come and stay at mine?'

Rose tried to ignore the tone of April's voice and hurried on. 'Please, just for a few nights. I'd be so grateful.'

'What's wrong with your apartment?'

'Look, I can't talk about it over the phone. Can I come and stay or not?' *Please, please say yes.*

'I have no idea what's going on with you, but if that's what you want, then come round. I'm working from home today, so I'll be in whenever you arrive.'

'Thank you, April. You've no idea what this means to me.'

Rose was cut off before she'd finished the sentence. April had made it very clear she didn't want her company, but she was desperate. The hotel was too expensive to stay in for more than a few nights, and she wasn't ready to go home. She might never be ready to go home.

She phoned Ben to tell him where she'd be. They had been out for dinner together and seen a film since their first date. He'd walked her back to the hotel.

'I know it's weird, me paying for a hotel when I've got a perfectly good flat, but I can't stay there right now,' she'd told him.

'I understand. It's a normal response to having your home invaded,' he said. 'It's not a permanent solution, though. Have you thought about getting some counselling?'

'I don't know. I might. But right now, I just want to be able to sleep at night and work during the day. If I can't sort this out by myself, then I promise I'll get help.'

They kissed on the step of the hotel and shared a smile. Rose was more in love with Ben every day, and he with her.

She packed her suitcase quickly. The hotel laundry service meant her clothes were clean and pressed. She didn't need to take more to April's. She promised herself it would only be another few days then she'd go home. A few nights of good sleep. Then she'd feel more like tackling her problem.

April opened the door and gestured her in. Her flat was as neat as ever. Rose plonked her suitcase in the hall. April pointedly picked it up and stowed it in the guest bedroom. Rose wondered how many guests April ever had to stay.

'You can sleep in here.' April pushed open the door wide.

It was a pleasant room with a varnished wooden floor, a single bed with a cream duvet and pillows, and an oak wardrobe and matching bedside cabinet.

'It must be lovely having a spare room,' Rose said, trying to make suitable conversation.

What was she doing here? She and April had nothing in common. They never sought each other out or met separately from the group. As far as she knew, Goldie and Lily didn't either. April met all of them or none.

'I haven't much use for it. I store things here mainly.'

There wasn't evidence of storage. Rose's gaze swept the room. Perhaps April's wardrobe was stacked full. She made a mental note not to open its doors.

'How long will you be staying?' April asked.

'Look, I'm sorry, I know I'm putting you out and I want you to know that I'm eternally grateful.'

April nodded and went towards the kitchen. Rose followed her.

'Tea?'

'Have you got coffee?'

April filled the kettle and measured out spoonfuls of coffee. Rose watched, trying to structure what she'd say.

'Why me?' April said suddenly.

'Pardon?'

'Why me? Why not ask Lily if you can stay with her? Or even Goldie. Wrapped as she is in her wedding, she's got a big living room couch that has a pull-out bed. So why me?'

'I'm sorry, I should go.' Rose leapt up, spilling the mug of coffee that April had put in front of her. 'Forget I called, please.'

'Don't be silly, Rose,' April said sharply, pushing her shoulders until Rose had no choice but to sink back into her chair. 'I'm not saying you can't stay; I'm simply trying to understand why you'd choose me to phone. You and I aren't exactly close, are we?'

Rose didn't reply.

'I'm your last resort,' April said. 'Okay, I get it.'

'Sorry.'

'Stop apologising. Anyway, you can stay. I won't be in much; I've got a ton of work on.'

'Don't you want to know why I'm here?'

'I assumed you'd tell me if you wanted to.'

Rose fiddled with the mug until April took it away from her. She noticed April was taking deep breaths in and out.

'Are you okay?' Rose asked.

April looked embarrassed. 'I have breathing exercises to do. This isn't about me, it's about you. Are you ready to tell me what's going on?'

Rose told her about the break-in and how she couldn't sleep. She told her about the nightmares and her fear the intruder would return. April sat and listened without interrupting. Rose was glad. If it was Lily, she'd be jumping up and hugging Rose and pouring out sympathy. If it was Goldie, she'd be asking lots of questions and making a list of what had gone wrong and where the positives might lie. April did nothing. She wasn't invested in Rose the way her other friends were.

'And that's that, really,' Rose trailed off lamely.

April still sat there. Rose squirmed on her seat. Was she being judged? Then April got up. She looked at Rose. 'There are towels in the bathroom cupboard and packets of soap. Help yourself.'

'That's it? You're not going to give me advice or help me?' Rose said.

'I am helping you,' April said. 'I'm giving you a place to stay until you get your head together.'

'What about the nightmares? How do I get past those?'

'I don't know. Look, I'm no expert, and that's why I won't give you advice. That would be wrong.'

'You could say something comforting,' Rose cried. 'Most people would.'

'Go home and see your mother if you want comfort. Here, all I can offer is my spare room.'

Rose thought about that. Very well, she'd take April's version of help. April's jibe about her mother had hit home. Rose knew she had to make that visit. But not yet. She wasn't ready for that lonely, empty house. She was being selfish. Her mother had to live there with Rose's Dad's absence. A little more time, that was all Rose asked for.

'What's wrong with your hands?' She noticed April's posture.

★　★　★

April didn't want Rose there. Her plea had come out of the blue, but it was too rude to say no. After all, Rose was her friend. April knew she should be more generous, but it was hard letting even a friend into her personal space.

Her home was her sanctuary. But with Rose there, it'd be different. There'd be no peace and quiet. Rose would chat. She'd make noises and take up room. April would have to wait to use her own shower or bath. She'd have share meals and actually talk instead of eating and reading.

Having listened to Rose's story, she was sympathetic. That was why Rose could stay. She was frightened. April wasn't going to turn her back on that. The problem wasn't just Rose. On April's answer phone, the green light blinked. There were five messages from

Rachael. Hence her shaky hands.

She concentrated on her breathing, the way the doctor had told her to. It wasn't working. She clenched her hands into fists. That stopped them. Until she released her grip.

'April?'

Rose was looking at her with concern. April smiled.

'It's nothing, really. I've had a bit of stress with work and other things, and the doctor's told me to do these breathing exercises and mindfulness.'

'And are you?'

April shook her head. 'I'm not sure the breathing is helping.'

'You can't expect a miracle over-night,' Rose said. 'You have to keep at it. What about physical exercise? That's supposed to help.'

April glanced at her ceiling involun-tarily. It was all quiet now, but her neighbour was right. The floorboards did creak twice a week for an hour at a time. This was followed by laughter and low chat as his visitors filed past her door and out. She kept out of his way.

The phone rang. April made no move to pick it up. It rang out for nine and then the voicemail went on.

'Hi, this is April. I'm not here right now, so leave a message.'

'April? April? Oh for goodness sake, I know you're there. Why won't you speak to me? This isn't fair. I'm your only sister and you treat me like dirt. The money's gone, April. It's not about me, it's about Mum. I can't afford to buy all the groceries on what I earn. You know that . . . April? Pick the phone up. Pick it up!'

April pressed her fingers to her ears to block out Rachael's screeching voice. Rose got up and switched the phone off. They sat in blessed silence for a little while. Finally Rose spoke gently.

'How long has this been going on?'

'Since they moved out of town. While they were in Mayborough, I was living with them. Which meant I controlled the weekly budget and made sure Rachael gave her shar of her wages

165

over. Mum doesn't work now because of her ailments, so it's even harder for them. I know it's hard for them.'

'But Rachael makes it harder than it has to be?' Rose guessed.

April nodded. 'She spends her money on clothes and makeup and then can't understand when there's not enough left over to buy essentials at the end of the week. Mum's no better. They can't manage. Or they could if only they'd just work it out.'

'Instead, they call you. Are you bankrolling them?'

'I give what I can but it's never enough. I don't want Mum to miss eating proper meals, but I can't make Rachael see that she needs to save and not squander.'

'No wonder you're stressed. You've got your business to run as well. You'd have to be a superwoman to manage all that without falling apart.'

April looked at Rose as if seeing her for the first time. She saw the compassion in her friend's dark eyes.

'You've too much on your plate and I'm not helping matters,' Rose said. 'I can't stay here.'

'It's funny, but I think this is the first real conversation you and I have ever had.' April smiled and the action felt strange, like she hadn't smiled for a very long time. 'I don't want you to go.'

'If I stay, then I can help in some way. I could make the meals. That might take some of the burden off you,' Rose said eagerly.

'Let's see how we go,' April said. 'You're only here for a few days.'

Rose took out her mobile and waved it in front of April. 'We can start with me ordering a takeaway for tonight's dinner. Do you like Indian or Chinese food?'

There was a creak of wood from the ceiling. They both looked up. April checked her watch.

'Excuse me, I need to go out for an hour. Help yourself to drinks and borrow a book, if you like.'

Ignoring Rose's bemused stare, April

went out into the hall, closing her door behind her. Her hand hovered over the door to the upstairs conversion. She argued with herself silently. She had to acknowledge that the breathing exercises alone weren't helping. The leaflet suggested yoga was excellent for relieving stress. Her decision had nothing to do with Steve's good looks. It was just yoga.

She knocked. She heard the sound of footsteps coming down and almost ran back into her own home. Steve looked surprised, and then pleased, to see her.

'April Lyons, my elusive downstairs neighbour. How are you?'

'I'm good,' she lied.

'You're coming to my yoga class? Come on up. The others will be here soon.' He bounded up the stairs not waiting to see if she was going to follow.

His upper half of the house was laid out like hers. Except instead of wood flooring, oak furniture and cream walls, he had carpets and wall hangings and an ornate ceiling lamp. An enormous canvas of red and yellow splashes took up one wall of his living room. April liked it. It was odd but strangely beautiful.

There was no time to speak to Steve before the others arrived. There was an older couple, both grey-haired and conventionally dressed. April didn't think they looked the kind to do yoga. When they took off their jackets, she was startled to see they both wore lycra. Steve's last group member was a pale young woman who was very slender with a nose ring and a long pale gold plait down her back.

Was she Steve's girlfriend? April watched as the group settled cross-legged on mats. Steve had given her one. He didn't seem to treat the pale woman any differently from the rest. April tried to sit cross-legged and found her knee joints stiff and painful.

'This is my downstairs neighbour, April, who's joining us this evening.'

There was a murmur of greetings.

Then Steve turned on the music and began to stretch. April copied the others as best she could. It was a gruelling hour. By the end, she was sensing muscles she didn't know she owned. She ached all over. Her knees were sore and she'd stubbed a toe.

In spite of that, she felt . . . *better*. As if a weight had lifted, even if only for a moment. The couple put on their jackets. The pale woman lifted her bag and the three said goodbye and left. April was about to go to when Steve stopped her.

'How did you find that?'

'It was good.' She felt she needed to say more. 'Thank you.'

He looked amused. 'You're welcome. I hope you'll come to the next session. It's very informal, so pop up if you can.'

'Thank you,' she repeated.

'Bob and Mary, the couple who come, they liked you, I can tell. It's difficult to tell with Tamara; her head's in the clouds, but I'm sure she did too. There's a good vibe in the group

170

— you're bringing balance.'

April didn't fully understand him, but she liked listening to him talk. He had a rich southern accent. She liked the flecks of gold running through his beard. He had a cute way of nodding to emphasise his points.

'Do you want to stay and eat? I've got pasta and I can whip up a mean salad.'

'No, I can't. I can't stay. Thanks. My friend's downstairs waiting for me.'

'Sure, sure. Not to worry.' He nodded.

She turned to leave, hesitated, and turned back.

'Actually, Steve, Rose and I are getting a takeaway. Would you like to join us?'

★　★　★

'You left those kittens. I know you did. Why, Mum?'

Lily was standing in the kitchen of her parents' home at the Mansion House Hotel. The bright yellow school

171

minibus was parked outside. Theoretically she was at work, but she'd made a last-minute detour after dropping a group of boarding pupils for a day out. She always felt sorry for those who had to stay at school over the holidays, but it did keep her in work.

Margery Smith looked guilty. 'How did you find out it was me?'

'I looked at the writing on the cardboard box. It's a supplier you use at the hotel frequently. It was an educated guess. So?'

'I found them in one of the outhouses on the property. First I found two black ones and I thought that was all, so I left them for you. But a few days later, I checked and there were four more. I don't know where they'd hidden or where the mother was. We do have feral strays coming over from the farm across the way.'

'Why didn't you come in and say hello to me? You could've talked to me about the kittens.'

'I didn't want to bother you. You

don't come to visit us very much and I suppose I thought you might not want to see me.'

'Oh, Mum, that's not true.' Lily ran forward and gave her mother a hug.

At first, Margery's body was rigid, but Lily held on until she felt her mum soften and her arms go round her. Lily gently pulled away.

'I don't visit much because you and Dad are always so busy. It feels like I'm intruding.'

'We are incredibly busy,' Margery sighed. 'You have no idea what it takes to run such a large hotel and do it well.'

'Agreed.'

There was an uncomfortable silence. This was a contentious topic between them that was like a stick bobbing on the sea and refusing to sink. Margery and Hugh had wanted Lily to train in hotel management and to start by working at the hotel for experience. They had been very upset when Lily went her own way and was hired by the school.

'I'd love to see you, and I'd love it if you came to visit me and I could show you my home and my animals. Will you do that, please?' Lily said.

'Now that you've asked and I'm certain you'd like that, then we will. Now, what's the problem with the kittens? Are they sick?'

'No, nothing like that. They're all full of bounce. But I can't keep them, Mum. I can't afford to keep them.'

'Oh dear. I hadn't thought that one through. I'm so sorry. What will you do with them?'

'I'll have to advertise them or take them to a pet shop, I suppose.'

'I should have done that in the first place.' Margery frowned.

'Why did you bring them to me?'

'I knew you'd care about them.'

'And I do. I love them, but they need food and vet care as well.'

'Then I'll pay for that,' Margery said with a sudden smile at her daughter. 'Will you allow me to do that?'

'Mum, you really are a big softie,

aren't you?' Lily laughed.

'Maybe I am, but let's keep it between ourselves. I do have standards to maintain.' Margery smiled back. Then she became serious. 'Do you think your brother is doing the right thing, marrying this Goldie?'

Lily leapt to Goldie's defence. 'He couldn't do any better. Goldie's beautiful and kind and very organised. She'll make him a great wife.'

'We invited them over to sample the wedding menu recently. I find her very hard to get to know. I know she didn't like the food, and I did offer to make a different meal, but she didn't want that either. I was rather confused. I think your father put his foot in it too.'

'What did Dad do?' Lily could quite imagine her father doing it all wrong. He breezed along in life, assuming everyone liked things the way he did.

'He offered James and his fiancée the dowager flat here after they're married. It's a very generous gift, but she didn't like it.'

'Goldie said that?' Lily was astounded.

Margery shook her head. 'She didn't say it outright, but I could tell by her expression. I don't understand. I thought she'd be delighted. It's not many young couples that get a free first house as a wedding present.'

'Oh dear,' was all that Lily managed.

Poor Goldie. Lily saw it from both sides. Her parents thinking they were doing something kind for their son and his soon-to-be wife. While Goldie would think them overbearing. She liked her independence.

'Will James be happy?' Margery was asking worriedly.

Lily didn't have an answer to that one.

10

'Right, so I've got my sensible shoes on. Will these do?' Goldie asked.

Lily gave them the once-over and nodded. 'Very good. Not a stiletto or glitz in sight. You'll be fine in these.'

'I wasn't sure what to wear, so I've allowed myself some glamour.'

Goldie pirouetted, and her pretty summer dress with its flounces swung out around her in a cloud of silk.

'Glamour is allowed, but bring a wrap or cardigan.'

'Oooh, mysterious,' Goldie teased. 'Am I still not allowed to know where we're going for my hen party?'

'You'll find out soon enough,' came the answer as Lily picked up Goldie's clutch bag and the wrap she'd thrown on her bed. 'Come on, time to go.'

Lily was picking Goldie up at her flat, and when they came downstairs and out onto the street, Goldie gasped in amazement. There was a pink stretch limo waiting on the kerbside. The windows were tinted so she couldn't see inside, but when she appeared, the door was flung open and Rose and April waved and grinned.

Then the driver door opened and the chauffeur came out. He was wearing a grey uniform and a peaked cap.

'Hey, is he allowed here tonight?' Goldie said sharply. 'I thought it was a girls-only party.'

Lily squinted at her. 'What's the problem? I can't drive as I have champagne to drink in the limo with you, and Bryce offered to take us.'

Goldie found it hard to meet his eyes. Bryce touched the rim of his hat in mock salute and slid back behind the wheel.

'What was that all about?' Lily asked, her eyebrows raised in astonishment.

'Oh, it's nothing,' Goldie mumbled. 'Can we go already?'

'This is going to be fun,' Lily assured

her, and then gave her a push in to the limo.

Inside, it was as spacious as Goldie had imagined it would be. There was a bar and four flutes of champagne fizzing. Lily handed her one and told her to sit.

'What? You get to boss me about all evening?' Goldie sat where ordered.

'If it's necessary. Remember, I'm the chief bridesmaid, so I get to conduct all ceremonies this evening,' Lily told her, taking a rather large gulp of champagne and then sneezing.

They all giggled. April raised her glass in a toast. 'Here's to Goldie on her last days of freedom as a single woman.'

'Here's to Goldie,' they all chimed and raised their glasses.

'This is wonderful,' Rose said. 'I've never been in a stretch limo before.'

'We'll hire one for you when you and Ben get hitched,' Goldie teased. 'Do you think you guys will get married?'

'We've only just met,' Rose protested, but her pink cheeks showed her pleasure at the thought of marrying her lovely Ben.

'Where are we going, Lily?' April asked, and Rose threw her a grateful look at the change in subject. 'You haven't told any of us the exact plans.'

'That's because I didn't want the secret to get out. Don't worry, we aren't driving too far. Just far enough that we have time for another round of champagne. Who wants a top-up?'

With refilled glasses, the four friends sank back into the luxury of the limousine and let Bryce glide them along the country lanes. The roof of the limo was open, and they could hear the rush of the air and the chirps of birdsong. The occasional leaf floated in as they drove under the trees on the narrow roads.

Goldie was perfectly content and more than a little excited. She loved being with her friends, and going on a magical mystery tour was her idea of heaven. Okay, she'd have liked it even better if she was in charge with her notebook and lists, but so far Lily had done a great job. What was coming next?

Soon the limo came to a stop. April opened the door and stepped out. The others followed. Bryce came round.

'Sorry, I forgot I'm the chauffeur and should have opened the door for you ladies.'

'Now you're here, you can carry the picnic hamper,' Lily told him, pointing back to the interior. 'Don't forget the other bottle of champagne, please.'

'You're a hard task master,' Bryce grumbled good-naturedly as he vanished into the limo and returned with a huge wicker hamper and a bottle under his arm. 'Okay, where to now?'

'Up there,' Lily said simply.

They all looked in the direction she was facing. They were in a small forestry car park, and there was a path leading off between the trees and heading steadily uphill. There was a collective groan.

'That's why I told you to wear stout

footwear.' Lily grinned. 'We're going all the way to the top. Get started and I'll catch you up. There's one more thing I need to bring with us.' She dived back into the limo.

April shrugged. 'I suppose we have to do what we're told, but I have to say this is the strangest hen party I've ever been to. Mostly it's wine bars and clubs and lots of noise.'

'I like this better,' Goldie said, breathing in the sweet air and enjoying the green leafiness and woodland sounds. 'Shall we go? I don't want Lily to start marching us up here.'

Bryce led the way. Goldie stayed back, letting April and Rose go between them. She felt foolish, but after the way they'd parted, she was more than awkward around him. Their conversation had rung in her head over and over the past few days. Had she known how Bryce felt about her on a subconscious level? She couldn't answer that. Or did she not want to answer it truthfully?

Her head ached thinking about it.

She had been in love with Bryce back in high school. It had killed her to break up with him. But she'd known she had to do it. He wasn't serious about her. They were too young then. He was only going to cause her heart more pain if she stayed as his girlfriend. He'd gone off to university then, and she'd done a secretarial course at the local college.

Even if they had tried to stay together, it wouldn't have worked, she reasoned. Long-distance relationships seldom did. It was right that they let each other go. They needed their space as young people and the chance to meet other people. Just as she'd met James again when he finished university and came back to Mayborough to work for his father.

She'd known James from school, but they hadn't moved in the same circles of friends. She met him properly when she went to buy her first car once she got her first permanent job. He'd been so kind and attentive, and got her a really great deal. Then he'd asked her out. And Goldie had said yes.

He was everything she'd wanted. He was kind and polite and well bred. There was good chemistry between them. She found his parents too involved in his life, but told herself that would change as she and James became more serious about each other. Above all, she loved his sense of belonging. The Smiths had lived in Mayborough for generations. There was even a statue in the town square to a portly Victorian Smith who'd brought prosperity through owning mills and educating the poor. There were plenty of Smiths on the local war memorials who had laid down their lives for king and country.

Goldie loved that sense of history and roots as much as she loved James himself. Now, as she struggled up the path on the hillside, she had an uneasy question to ask herself. How much *did* she love James? Was it purely him that she loved? Or was it the culture and sense of belonging that went with him?

She shook the thoughts aside. She couldn't . . . she *wouldn't* go there. She was in love with James and they were getting married next week. For goodness sake, here she was on her hen night! That was how real it was. Nothing was going to change now.

Without wanting to, she remembered Bryce coming back to Mayborough. She'd been so surprised to bump into him a few years ago in the town. She'd imagined that once he graduated, he'd head to Europe or America to work. Instead, he'd had come home and worked for a company within commuting distance. Often he worked from his home office.

The reason he was home, he'd told her, was that his mother was poorly. Luckily, Morag's health had gradually improved over the following six months, and now she was very fit and healthy. Yet Bryce had stayed. Goldie was glad. She and Bryce had met up for coffees and lunches to chat as friends. She'd already been going out with James and it was getting serious. So, friendship was what she wanted. Bryce had seemed fine with that. He never hinted at more.

He was being incredibly unfair now, Goldie thought. No way could she have known how he felt about her. He'd kept it hidden. Only her needling had brought out the truth. She was about to marry another man. It was awful of Bryce to tell her he loved her. Awful.

Lily had caught up to her. She was carrying a long hold-all that looked suspiciously familiar.

'Isn't that my . . . ' Goldie began.

'Hush, ask no questions and you'll get no lies,' Lily whispered, overtaking her and striding out to the top of the hill.

Goldie puffed as she followed her. Thankfully, the ground began to flatten out. She'd arrived. The others were admiring the view. She looked about. It was a beautiful place. The trees had thinned, leaving wide vistas to the low fields and valleys below. She made out the sea, glittering to the west. There was Mayborough, looking like dolls' houses below. The sun was dipping now and the sky was a streaky aquamarine and lemon.

'The first stars are out,' Goldie said. 'There's Venus. How lovely she looks.'

She caught Bryce's gaze for a brief moment and looked away. There was something in his expression she didn't want to analyse. She'd make more effort, she promised herself. They'd still be friends. It didn't have to be awkward.

She smiled at him. 'I'm starving. Are we going to eat that?' She indicated the hamper on the ground beside him.

Bryce smiled back, and it was so normal that she let out a breath she hadn't known she was holding. It was going to be all right. He understood. He forgave her.

Lily clapped her hands. 'I'd like to say welcome to us all. We're here this evening to celebrate Goldie's last days as a singleton before she marries my big brother. We're going to eat delicious food from the hamper and open another bottle of fizz — but most of all, we're going to watch the best show of shooting stars the heavens can offer. Which is why I've brought Goldie's telescope.' She pulled it out of the hold-all with an elaborate flourish, and they all applauded.

Goldie felt ready tears prick the back of her eyes. She was so emotional these days. Lily had organised the perfect hen party for her. The Perseid showers of meteors was to be at its best tonight. To be honest, she'd been a little annoyed that her hen party was for this date and she'd miss them. How petty she'd been. And how thoughtful her friends were.

'Thank you all,' she said. 'This really is marvellous.'

'Bryce, please spread the picnic blanket. April, you open the hamper, and Rose you can help me set up the telescope. Goldie, you are to do nothing but sit and be pampered,' Lily bossed unashamedly.

They sat and spread out the food. There was smoked salmon, hardboiled eggs, crackers, party sausages and salad. There were also home-made scones with cream and jam sent by Morag. The sky was darkening steadily and more stars appeared by the minute.

'There's one,' Goldie shouted, almost choking on her egg. She leapt up and got to the telescope. 'Did you see it? A shooting star.'

'There's another,' April said. 'In fact, I'm sure we'll all see one. They bring luck, don't they?'

'They sure do,' Goldie laughed. 'You can cast a wish when you see one and it'll definitely come true.'

They were all watching intensely, and a shout went up when a shooting star went by. What was each of them wishing for? Goldie wished for her perfect Goldilocks wedding. Bryce's face was solemn: no clues to what he wished for, but she had an uncomfortable feeling she knew what it was. April stared at her hands and then at the sky.

Rose too, stared hard at the heavens and rubbed her arms.

When they finished the food and the meteor shower faded out, Lily suggested a walk in the woods. 'I brought torches,' she said, rummaging in the hold-all and bringing them out.

'We may have flashlights, but what about the hamper and my telescope?' Goldie asked.

'We'll carry those with us,' Bryce said. 'The hamper's empty; I can manage both. That's my job tonight: chauffeur, handy man and gofer.'

'Are we sure we want to walk in the woods at night?' Rose said. 'Isn't it a little spooky?'

'That's sort of the point,' Lily said. 'Besides, there's nothing here but badgers and foxes. And we've got Bryce to protect us.'

'Add bodyguard to my list of duties,' he joked. When he saw Rose's tense face, he added, 'Lily's right, any noises will be animals foraging. There's nothing to be scared about.'

'The most danger is the fact we've all had several glasses of fizz,' April remarked drily. 'Look out for the tree roots.'

Which proved to be prescient. It was April who stumbled and fell after catching her foot in the roots of a giant oak. She cried out and lay where she fell. Bryce hurried back and helped her up. She cried out again when she tried to stand up.

'It's my foot. It's painful. I can't put any weight on it.'

They all huddled round her, concerned.

'I think you've twisted your ankle,' Bryce said once he'd examined it by torchlight. 'A trip to A & E is in order to check it out. I don't believe it's broken, but better safe than sorry.'

The limo was an odd sight, parked in the hospital car park at midnight amongst ordinary cars and a line of ambulances. It took up more than its fair share of space. Bryce half carried April inside, despite her protests.

Goldie, Lily and Rose followed.

'I feel guilty. This is all my fault,' Lily said.

'It's not your fault. It was an accident, that's all,' Goldie said.

'It was a gorgeous hen party,' Rose said. 'April's fall wasn't predictable. She might have fallen anywhere or tripped on the pavement outside her house. She isn't going to blame you. We were all so happy tonight.'

Lily's face brightened. 'Thanks you two. I love you both so much. I only hope April's okay.'

Bryce came back after a long while to say that April had indeed twisted her ankle and the doctor was strapping it up. She wouldn't be long. Rose and Lily rushed off to find her in the treatment room. Goldie rose, intending to go with them, but Bryce held her back.

'We have to talk,' he said in a low voice.

The waiting room was busy and no one was listening in to them.

Goldie kept her own voice quiet and

measured. 'We don't need to talk. We're friends, right? You told me that after the kayaking. You said you'd always be my friend.' There was a wobble in her tone and she wished it'd go away.

'That's just it, Goldie. Once you're married, we can't be friends. It's not right. You and James deserve to be together with no ex-boyfriends in the background. Let's face it, men and women aren't meant to be friends.'

'That's not true,' she whispered.

But Bryce strode past her and out into the night.

11

'Ouch, ouch and ouch again.' April stumbled on her crutches and gave an impatient cry.

'Here, sit down and let me get you some breakfast,' Rose said, leaping up from her own bowl of cereal to guide April to the chair.

'This is simply ridiculous,' April growled. 'My ankle is only twisted, not broken, so why is it so awfully sore? And why do I need these equally ridiculous contraptions?' She jabbed at the crutches.

Rose put a bowl of cereal in front of her and slid over the jug of milk. 'The doctor said it was a bad sprain and will take up to six weeks to heal, didn't she? You have to have patience. As for the crutches, can you walk without them?'

April muttered under her breath and Rose hid a smile. No prizes for guessing that April would make the worst patient ever.

'I'm glad you're here,' April said. 'I'm not sure how I'd manage without help right now.'

Rose kept her gaze on her bowl. How was she going to tell her friend that she planned to leave? She couldn't keep living with April while her own flat lay empty. Ben had kindly checked in her place regularly, but Rose knew she had to face up to her life soon. Besides, she had come to an important decision.

Suddenly, she knew she had to tell April. It wasn't fair to hold it back. 'Actually, April . . . ' she began, ' . . . there's something I need to say.'

'Hmmm?' April was picking out the raisins in her cereal and laying them to one side on a plate.

Rose coughed and swallowed. She tried again and found her voice stronger and more confident. 'I'm sorry; I was going to tell you this after Goldie's hen party, but then we had the trip to the hospital and getting you home and so on.'

'Tell me what?' The raisin sorting halted. Milk dripped from April's cereal spoon.

'I told you about the nightmares I had after the break-in.'

'Yes, you did. Are you still getting them? I thought you were sleeping better since you moved in here?'

Rose nodded. 'I am sleeping better. But I do have a few nightmares, only they've changed. They're not about an intruder anymore. They're . . . they're about my dad. About losing him. The dream starts with me as a child. It's always the same dream. I'm wearing a blue gingham dress with white ankle socks and black patent leather shoes. My hair's in pigtails. I can feel it flicking against my face as I skip along between Mum and Dad. We're going on a picnic and we're walking through a wildflower meadow. Mum puts down a picnic blanket and we sit and get our sandwiches. Dad's chatting to me. Then

I look over at the horizon and see a cloud like a ball, black as night; and as I watch, it gets bigger and bigger until it fills the sky. I'm screaming, and I look around for Mum and Dad, and they're gone. They're gone, April. I feel so utterly terrified and alone, and I'm running in the field but there's nothing there. Then at this point, I usually wake up.'

Her hands were clammy even describing the nightmare. She dug her fingernails into her palms.

'It's only a dream,' April said, ever the practical one. 'Anyway, that's why you're staying with me, isn't it? It'll be worse at your flat if you're on your own.'

'I think it's a message from my subconscious. I think I need to go home.'

'Go home? You mean to your flat?'

'No, I mean I need to go home to see my mum. I've been putting it off for too long. I've been terribly selfish and I have to put it right.'

197

'You're going to London?'

'I'm going to London on the late train this evening. Sorry, I should've told you, but I couldn't really because I've only made my mind up. I can't leave you here struggling along, so I'm going to ask Steve to drop in on you and help if he can.'

'You can't do that.' April sounded horrified.

Rose smiled. 'Steve's a lovely bloke. Besides, I've already told him about your accident, and he said if he could help in any way he'd love to.'

'I don't have much choice, do I?' April sniffed.

'Please don't be like that,' Rose begged. 'I don't want to leave when you need looking after, but I have to do this. Can you understand that?'

April poked at the soggy pile of raisins. Then she sighed and nodded. 'The trouble is, I've got used to having company. I never imagined I'd like it.'

'I'm very grateful to you for letting me stay. I knew it'd be hard for you, but

I was so desperate.'

'Is Ben going to London with you?'

'He asked if I wanted him to, but I need to go alone.'

She didn't tell April that Ben had then kissed her so wonderfully that she felt dizzy, and was even more certain, if that was possible, that she'd fallen in love with him. She felt safe and strong when she was with him, and he made her heart sing. Ben had asked her again if he should travel to London with her. But Rose knew she had to battle her demons alone. She had to stop being so afraid.

'Enough about me,' Rose said. 'I haven't asked how you are. I mean, apart from the ankle. How are your hands? Your breathing?'

'Maybe you should just ask if Rachael's phoned again,' April said drily.

'Has she?'

'Luckily no. Perhaps that has something to do with the fact that I posted another cheque a few days ago.'

'Did the yoga work for you?'

'It's helping. Steve showed me a few moves I can do here. Well, I did do them, but clearly I can't now until my ankle's healed. Gosh, look at the time; I need to get going. I have to shower and dress and then hobble down to the office. Sally needs an eye kept on her, and I've missed one day there.' April got up painfully and managed to get her crutches in place under her arms. 'I hope it goes well in London. Let me know when you get back.'

'I will,' Rose said with a smile.

She watched April's departing back as she hobbled along the corridor to the bathroom. It was strange how close she felt to her friend now. They almost understood one another!

* * *

It took rather longer than her usual five minutes for April to walk to her warehouse. The crutches weren't good on uneven ground, and cobblestones were a nightmare. They chafed her arms and rubbed the skin between her thumb and forefinger until she was convinced she had blisters.

She tried to hurry but had to slow when she nearly fell into the road. Forced to walk slowly and carefully, she tried to calm her mind. It was difficult when she wasn't sure what was happening at work. She hadn't had a day off in years. She had to be in charge and keep a very close eye on Sally and Lucy to make sure everything was just as she needed it to be.

How had they coped without her? April sent up a silent prayer that Sally hadn't made any bold decisions. As for Lucy, she wondered if she'd made a mistake in hiring her. The girl often made errors and seemed quite forgetful. Probably mooning over some boy or other half the time.

She got there in the end after what felt like years.

'Oh, what have you done to yourself?' Sally gasped.

'Please don't fuss,' April said abruptly. 'It's nothing. I fell and twisted my ankle.'

'You poor thing. Is it very painful? Should you be at work? Lucy and I can hold the fort, you know.'

'Of course I should be at work. Where else would I be? Please bring me the day's schedule. Oh, and tell Lucy I want to look over the books, so tidy them up before I get my computer up and running. I'd have checked them on my laptop at home if I hadn't been so distracted with my ankle.'

She didn't bother to wait and see if Sally was following orders. Focusing on her blisters and the clumsy crutches, she turned and headed for her office. Really, it would be a whole lot easier if she could run her business on her own. Relying on other people was annoying. Their standards were never quite up to scratch.

Inside, she sat down thankfully. Then, after a few minutes, she powered up her computer and prepared to read her long list of emails. Some were spam and easily deleted. Most were orders or enquiries about cakes and other bakery items. April did, on occasion, make other sweets apart from cakes, if the price was right.

She ran through in her head what she had to do. Thank goodness Goldie's wedding cake was all made up and ready to go. The actual construction of the three tiers would happen in place at the Mansion House Hotel on the big day, of course, but it was satisfying to know that the three tiers were made and iced. April didn't want to imagine trying to do that with her ankle the way it was. Could she even balance well enough to ice cakes today?

At least her hands weren't shaking so much these days. The breathing exercises and mindfulness were paying dividends. Steve's yoga moves helped too. Her mind drifted from the emails about cake enquiries to her upstairs neighbour. He had turned out to be a very entertaining conversationalist.

He'd accepted her spontaneous invitation to share the takeaway with herself and Rose, even though as soon as she said it she wanted to take it back.

He'd chatted easily with Rose about photography, confessing to taking snaps as a hobby with an old pre-digital camera he owned. Rose had been animated and asked to see it. Steve had nipped upstairs and brought his camera and some of his photos down, and even April had been interested in it all. It turned out Steve had travelled a good deal, and his photos were of exotic locations such as Vietnam, Thailand and Borneo.

When they finished discussing photography, Steve had asked what April did for a living. He'd been fascinated by her stories of cakes baked and sold to the famous and not-so-famous. She'd been persuaded to provide cake as dessert after their takeaway curries, and Steve had said how delicious it was.

She liked him. There — she'd said it, if only to herself. That didn't mean she wanted to date him. But there was no harm in being friends.

April frowned as her eye caught a new email fresh in. Then she stood and as quickly as she could manage, went to the office door and shouted for Sally. Her assistant arrived, red in the face and covered in flour dust.

'What's the matter, April? Is it your leg? Do you need me to help you?'

April shook her head impatiently. 'Why have I received a complaint from Mr Hedges? He writes that he ordered a cream cake for delivery yesterday but it didn't arrive. How is that possible? We *never* get complaints. I pride myself on it. What have you done?'

Sally shrank under the verbal attack. April waited, quietly seething. This was what happened when you took one day off work. Things slipped and got shoddy.

'I didn't want to disturb you when you were having a day off. But one of the ovens wasn't working and I had to get someone in to fix it. Then we were behind schedule, and you weren't there either to bake or decorate . . . ' She shrugged helplessly. 'It couldn't be avoided. I'll send a complimentary cream cake to Mr Hedges.'

'What a load of feeble excuses,' April shouted. 'It's not good enough, do you hear me? This is my business and I've a reputation to uphold. You don't have to worry about brand quality as you work for me. It's not your name that's going to be bandied about as not good enough!'

There was a terrible silence. April realised she'd gone too far and opened her mouth to say something. She wasn't sure what. About how they'd work late tonight and sort it all out. She didn't get the chance, though.

Sally's face was white. Her mouth trembled, but she slowly and deliberately took off her flour-dusted apron and dropped it on April's desk. April stared in astonishment.

'I've had enough,' Sally said, and her quiet, even tone chilled April to the bone. 'I've put up with your rudeness and your way of shutting me out for too long. I put up with it because I genuinely believe in this business, and I thought — I hoped — I was a part of it. But I'm leaving.'

Without another word, she walked away, leaving April with her mouth open.

⋆ ⋆ ⋆

Rose sat at a window seat on the evening train with a cup of takeaway coffee on the table in front of her. She'd eaten some rubbery chicken and chips from one of the fast food places at Mayborough railway station for dinner despite having little appetite. Now she took up her mobile and texted her mum to say she was popping down for a quick visit.

She stared out the window as the trees and countryside passed by in a verdant blur. Her ears were pricked for an answering text, but it didn't come.

She wasn't surprised. Rose's mum wasn't one for much modern technology. She had a mobile — for emergencies, as she'd told Rose — but didn't use it apart from that.

I could phone her, she thought. *But then I'd have to speak, and we'd get into all sorts of topics I'd rather talk to her about face to face.* She took a sip of her coffee. It wasn't too bad. It perked her mood. *I can do this. I can do this.* The train rattled along.

She arrived in London late and took a cab straight to her mother's door. Her parents had moved here only five years ago when her dad had got a promotion. Rose's mum had taken a job as a salesperson in a toy shop and had written to Rose telling her how much she loved it.

Her mum didn't speak when she saw Rose at her door; she simply rushed forward and crushed her in a giant hug. Rose felt kisses on her forehead and she hugged her mum fiercely.

'You didn't tell me you were coming

down, you naughty girl.'

'I texted you.'

'Oh, well, that was a nonsense doing that. You know I never read the blooming things. How are you? You're looking a bit peaky. Are those dark circles under your eyes? Too many late nights, is it?'

Rose followed her mum through into her living room. It was an explosion of colour. There were framed pictures of fairy-tale scenes on the walls, red and yellow throws on the couches and a scattering of fabrics, silk threads, measuring tapes and other sewing equipment.

'Mum, what's all this?'

'It's the tapestry banner I was telling you about. I'm making a start on it. Do you like the colours? Wait here — I've a bottle of lovely white wine in the fridge, and I'm sure I can rustle up some olives and cheese.'

Rose waited. She heard her mother slamming a fridge door and the pop of a wine bottle cork. She heard the clink of glasses and rustling as food was unwrapped. And she felt her dad's absence. He should've been at the door welcoming her in. He'd had a hearty, booming voice that filled a room and a wonderful laugh that made everyone want to join in. She rubbed furiously at her nose. She wasn't going to cry.

'How's work?' she called through, determined to be all right.

'It's pretty good, actually,' her mum called back. 'Do you want any pickled onions?'

She came back with a stacked tray. Rose helped her put the glasses and food on the low table, after clearing it of fabric samples.

'Rose,' her mum said, sounding so pleased that Rose's heart squeezed. 'Rose, darling, it's so lovely to see you. It's been ages.'

'It's been far too long, I know. That's why I'm here. I've neglected you, Mum. I . . . I didn't want to come here when Dad . . . when Dad isn't here. I've been horribly selfish, and you can say that to my face. You can, honestly.' Rose noticed that her cheeks were wet and touched them. She hadn't known she was crying. So much for promising herself that she wouldn't.

'I know that's why you haven't visited. I'm not going to lie. It's been hard living here without him, but it's got easier, and it'll get easier for you too, pet. Each visit will be better. Will you try? I do miss you.'

'You'd better get me a resident toothbrush and space in the toiletries cupboard,' Rose joked, 'because I'm going to be coming down a lot. There's been some stuff happening to me which I'll tell you about over supper, but I've realised I need to stand up to it and not run away from my problems.'

'That's my girl.'

'Did I tell you about Goldie's hen party?' Rose asked, feeling all at once warm and cosy and very content. She dried her face, blew her nose on the proffered paper hanky, and propped a couple of cushions behind her.

Her mother smiled and settled herself more firmly on the couch opposite. She picked up the plate of food and offered it to Rose.

'Olives? Now, once you've got that down you, I want to hear all about Goldie's hen party and the plans for the wedding.'

12

'You have to go and apologise to her,' Rose said.

April had been home, fretting about work, when Rose arrived back from London looking brighter than she'd seen her for a long while. April immediately told her about the blow-up with Sally. It was odd how she'd come to rely on Rose's good sense and friendship. April knew she'd miss her when she moved out.

'I find it very hard to say I'm sorry.'

Rose grinned. 'Yes, we all know that from past experience, but we love you anyway. But Sally deserves it. She works very hard for you and she's a nice, kind person. You'd be a fool to let her get away. Do you want her working for another bakery?'

'No, I certainly don't. Sally's half the reason for my success.'

'Then tell her that. Don't delay. In fact, I'll fetch your jacket and drive you over to her house myself, right now.'

April, for once, let herself be commanded. She put on her cotton jacket, brushed her hair and refreshed her makeup. Her hands shook slightly as she applied her lipstick. She breathed in and out. She was anxious. There was no getting away from it. Sally was furious with her. How would she react when April appeared on her doorstep?

Rose looked her up and down and pronounced her satisfactory. Then she drove her across to the new housing estate where Sally lived with her husband and two children. April hoped that the husband was out working and the kids playing with friends. She needed Sally alone.

Unexpectedly, Rose reached over and gently squeezed her hand. 'You're going to be fine. I'll wait here.'

'Thanks,' April said. 'I'm so glad you're here.'

Sally's face wasn't encouraging when

she saw April. She let her come in, though, as far as the hall.

'Is there somewhere more private we could speak?' April said, her mouth dry.

'This will do. No one else is home. What do you want?'

'I want to say sorry. I'm so sorry I said all those horrible things to you. I can't run the business without you, that's the truth.'

Sally's expression softened but she didn't speak. *Great*, April thought. *She's making me work for this. I deserve it, though*. 'Please, please come back to work.'

'I'll come back to work on one condition.'

'Anything. What is it?'

Sally smiled. 'You have to promise to talk to me. I mean really talk to me — about how it's going, how you're feeling, what you're doing. The sort of chat which makes a day flow by happily. I hate how silent and cut off you are.'

'Am I honestly that bad?' April said.

'Don't doubt it. I'm not asking you

to change your whole personality, just to open up a bit more, that's all.'

'I'll try. Will you come back now?'

Sally turned away.

'Where are you going?' April said, alarmed that she'd put Sally off somehow.

Sally turned back with her bag and waved it at her. 'Getting my stuff. Now are we going to work or aren't we?'

Rose dropped them both at the warehouse. She was pleased and relieved that April had sorted everything out with Sally. What April didn't understand was that she needed Sally. She acted as if she was all alone and didn't need people, but she did. Maybe April was beginning to learn that.

Rose was learning about herself too. Her few days at home had been a tonic. She had still felt the gap where her dad should've been, and that was painful. But her mum was making the most of life and was being incredibly positive. Some of it had rubbed off on

Rose. Surely, if Mum could do it, so could she?

They'd window-shopped and discovered little coffee houses for cake during the day. In the evenings they'd eaten takeaway and sewed the first scene of the fairy-tale tapestry banner. And they'd talked and talked. Much of their chat was memories, and many of those were about Rose's dad. They'd laughed and cried together.

Rose left with a promise, heartfelt, to come back regularly to visit. There was a plan for her mum to come to Mayborough in the autumn, and an idea they might go on holiday together at Christmas.

Now, Rose let herself in to April's home and gathered up her belongings. She'd enjoyed the safety of staying there, but it was time to go home. She decided she'd ring April that evening and thank her for her hospitality.

She parked in her usual space and stared up at the apartment block. She waited for the familiar sensation of dread, but it didn't come. The hallway was quiet as she reached her floor.

'Hello dear. You're back, then?' Mrs Dawson was coming out from her flat.

'Yes, I'm back now. I'm looking forward to being home,' Rose said, and knew it was true.

'Did you hear they caught the burglars?'

'That's fantastic news.' Rose felt a weight lifting, like another layer of pressure gone. 'How did they catch them?'

'It was a couple of young lads, not more than twenty. Imagine that. The police caught them red-handed breaking into houses not far from here. I'm very glad they have. My son Stanley's been visiting and checking on me, and he's so busy with his work and family that I feel quite guilty letting him. Now I don't have to worry about that. How are you, dear? Sleeping better?'

'I'm much better, thank you, Mrs Dawson. In fact, I feel one hundred percent improved. I must go now. My friend's getting married tomorrow, and I'm the official photographer. I have to prepare.'

'How lovely. There's nothing nicer than a summer wedding. I'm off to afternoon tea with Stanley and Sandra, so I'll see you later. I do like having you next door. It makes me feel so much better knowing you're there. Goodbye.'

Rose let herself in, thinking that she too was glad Mrs Dawson was her neighbour. They could look out for each other. Her mum would like Rose's neighbour, too; she could imagine them having interesting conversations over tea. When her mum came to visit, Rose thought, she'd ask Mrs Dawson round as well.

She was very glad the burglars had been caught. She didn't need to fear them coming back now. Her flat smelt of dust and undisturbed air. The first thing she did was fling the windows open. Then she got a duster and polish and cleaned every surface until the place smelt of lavender.

The gap where the television had been was very obvious. Rose decided she'd buy a new one soon. Although, now she and Ben were dating each other, she'd have less time to watch it. She'd be too busy having nights out at the cinema or for dinner. What a lovely thought.

She began to sort out her photography equipment, planning what she'd need for the next day. She couldn't quite believe Goldie was getting married. There had been such a buildup over the last few months, but the moment was almost here.

Her doorbell rang and she didn't jump out of her skin. It was progress. Rose grinned to herself. She knew who was at the door. She'd phoned Ben to let him know she was back. He had a day off and they were going to spend it together.

He greeted her with a long, passionate kiss which left her breathless.

'I missed you,' he said.

'I guessed. Thanks for checking on

my place while I've been at April's. Did you hear they caught the burglars?'

'Didn't you get my text? As soon as I heard, I let you know.'

'No, I didn't get it. Never mind, Mrs Dawson told me all about it, and I'm very happy with the news.'

'How was London? How was your mum?' Ben came in, took off his shoes and padded through to Rose's tiny kitchen to put the kettle on.

Rose thought how comfortable they were together. It was as if they'd known each other forever.

'London was awfully busy with tourists and Mum is fine. In fact, she's more than fine; she's making the most of her life. She's shown me that I need to do the same. Dad's gone, but that doesn't mean we'll forget him. We'll keep our memories alive and swop stories. Did I tell you Mum's going to come for a visit in October? I'm not sure where I'm going to put her yet as the flat's so small, but we'll manage.'

'I'm sure you'll manage. You're a strong woman, Rose Redd.'

Ben gathered her in his arms and kissed the top of her head. She leaned into him, hearing the steady beat of his heart. The kettle switch popped and they stood back. Ben made the tea and Rose found a few biscuits in her treat tin.

'These might be a bit hard on the teeth; I don't know how old they are. Biscuits don't go out of date though, do they?'

'Rose,' Ben said.

'What? You think these will make us sick? We don't have to eat them, I suppose.'

'Rose . . . can you be quiet about the biscuits, please?'

'Oh.'

'How do you feel being back in your flat? Will you sleep okay now?'

Rose lifted her shoulders. 'I'm really not sure. I haven't had the nightmares since the day I got to London. I don't think I'll mind sleeping here now that the villains have been caught. I have to try it and see.'

Ben took in a long, deep breath. 'I was wondering . . . I just thought that . . . '

'You want me to start talking about biscuits again?'

'No, no,' Ben said hurriedly. 'What I'm trying to say is, that if we got married, you wouldn't have to worry about being on your own.'

Rose put down the biscuit tin. The kettle made odd churring noises. Maybe it needed replacing. *Ben wanted to marry her. He was proposing to her.* Never mind the kettle and the mouldy biscuits. She was going to marry Ben!

'Rose?' Ben said, sounding afraid.

'The answer is yes. Yes, oh yes, oh yes, I will marry you, my lovely Ben.'

She reached up on tiptoe and kissed him thoroughly.

When they came down from the clouds, they decided to keep their engagement a secret until Goldie and James got married. It wasn't fair to take away from their friends' big day. Besides, Rose thought, she wanted to hug their secret to her and savour it.

They sat in Rose's living room, and Ben helped her organise her camera and make her plans for the next day. They kept stopping to kiss and grin at each other. They argued about where they'd live after they married. Rose's flat had the best view but Ben's was larger. Ben suggested a year travelling abroad. Rose thought about wedding dresses.

None of the details mattered. Rose simply wanted to be with Ben. The rest of their lives would slot into place. She was confident of that.

★　★　★

Steve came down to see April. She was back early from work. Sally had insisted on paying for a taxi and dropping April off at home. They were slightly behind on cake orders, but April had decided not to panic.

Usually she'd be completely stressed by now and insisting they work late, but not today. Today she was too relieved that Sally had forgiven her.

'We'll send some chocolate muffins with the late delivery cakes to make up for it,' she suggested to Sally.

Sally had smiled. 'That sounds nice. I can add some icing sugar dusting or cinnamon flavour to spice them up, make them special.'

'We won't make a habit of being late,' April added.

'Of course not. But sometimes things happen and it's best not to let it affect our health.'

April had told Sally about her anxiety, and her assistant had promised to keep an eye on her.

'Will you consider taking on more staff?' Sally asked.

'If business stays steady at this level, then yes, by autumn, I'd like to take on a couple of people. And I'd like you to train them, if you don't mind doing so.'

'Me?' Sally sounded pleased.

'You're so good with people, and we both know that I'm not. I'll only end up shouting at them or getting impatient.'

'You're not that much of a dragon,' Sally laughed.

'Anyway, I'd like it if you did train them. Will you think about it?'

'I don't need to think about it. I'd love to do that. Thanks, April.'

Steve arrived at her door just as she did.

'Let me help you with your bag.'

'Thanks; these crutches get in the way big time.'

One slipped and Steve caught it before it crashed to the floor. April got the door open and they managed inside in a flail of crutches, handbag and laptop bag.

'Whew, do you need all this stuff? It's heavy.'

'I can usually manage it, but this ankle is a pain, and not just literally.'

'Is it feeling any better?' Steve took her jacket and hung it on the peg.

'Some, but it's tender. Anyway,

enough about me. How are you?'

'I was reminded by Rose that I promised to help you, so here I am. What needs doing?'

April was a little hurt that Steve had to be reminded by Rose to help her. Was she so forgettable? Then she glanced at him and saw the humour twinkling in his eyes. Something churned in her stomach. A sensation of delight and excitement. She made a fuss of putting her laptop on the sideboard to distract herself.

'I'm fine, really. I can manage all by myself. I've lived alone for years and I'm independent. I like it that way.'

Steve shook his head. 'Nice try, April, but it won't wash with me.'

'What do you mean?'

'Beneath that iron exterior, there's marshmallow. No one is completely independent. We all need other people. Especially when we're ill or vulnerable.'

'I'm not ill or vulnerable,' April said, horrified at the idea someone thought of her that way.

Steve pointed at her bandaged leg.

'Oh, well, that. I'm not ill.'

'You've been suffering with anxiety.'

'I didn't tell you that. How did you find out? That's my personal, private information. You've no right . . . '

Steve hushed her gently and guided her to the sofa and made her sit. He sat too.

'Listen, I'd have worked it out for myself anyway from the yoga class, but Rose told me. She's worried about you. She asked me to help.'

'She shouldn't have bothered you.'

'She was right to. She also told me why you're anxious.'

'She told you about Rachael?'

April wasn't certain whether she was furious with Rose or strangely thankful that it had been shared. The burden was no longer hers alone. Rose understood why the whole situation with her sister and mother had caused her stress. April's guilt about her family had lessened with that.

'She did,' Steve was saying. 'And I

think I can help.'

'You *have* helped, with the yoga.'

'I haven't always been a yoga teacher.'

April realised she knew very little about Steve, other than he was gorgeous, lived upstairs and taught yoga, and had travelled a great deal. He was a few years older than her. Enough that he had to have a past. It just hadn't occurred to her. She could imagine him teaching yoga on his travels to pay for rent and food.

'I was an accountant before I gave it up for a change of career. I was a good one, too. Particularly when it came to communicating with difficult customers. I'd like to have a chat with your sister. Set some boundaries. If you'd like me to.'

This was a side of him she hadn't seen before. He had a calm but determined expression as if he'd take no nonsense.

'What I'd like to make Rachael realise is that I'm not an endless pit of money,' she found herself saying. She hadn't intended to be so open and honest, but now that she'd begun she couldn't stop. 'I'm happy to send them a cheque each month. I don't want my mum to go without because there isn't enough cash. But I don't want to have Rachael phoning me when they run out, as they always do, because I can't afford to keep paying. My business is thriving and I may expand, but I withdraw only a small salary at present. I have to invest in the business, you see, and I have to pay Sally and Lucy.'

Steve nodded. 'Okay, so that's what we agree with Rachael. You will send a cheque at the beginning of each month to cover essentials, and I'm sure it will be a generous amount. However, if she phones for more before the next month, then the payments will stop.'

'Does that come across too harshly?'

'Not at all,' Steve said firmly. 'It's a business transaction. You let me deal with Rachael.'

April gave him the number and then

went through into the kitchen so she didn't hear the conversation. She'd had enough of her sister's shouts and threats.

Half an hour later, Steve came through. He looked completely calm.

'And?' April prompted.

'And, it's done. She's accepted our terms.'

April pressed a kiss to his cheek spontaneously. Then backed off, appalled at herself. Steve gave her a slow and delighted smile. 'April Lyons, would you like to have dinner with me this evening?'

'Is that dinner as in friends?' That must be what Steve meant. April felt her cheeks burning.

'It's whatever you want. It could be as friends or it could be a date. Which is it to be?'

April gazed at him. He was a handsome man. He was a good friend, and he'd helped her. She didn't need a relationship. She certainly didn't want a boyfriend . . . did she? She'd always sworn not to get married or get emotionally involved with someone. But none of that was important now, somehow.

'Steve Godley, I'd love to have dinner with you this evening.'

Steve waited, his smile now hesitant.

April gave in. 'Yes, Steve, I'd very much like to go out on a date with you.'

⋆ ⋆ ⋆

Goldie was at the Mansion House Hotel. The wedding rehearsal at the church had gone well that morning. Dirk had done a great job of giving her away, choreographed by the vicar as if it was a dance. She had walked up the aisle to James. The vicar was calling instructions but Goldie didn't hear them. Instead of feeling happy, her muscles were tense and her jaw ached from holding a polite smile.

It hadn't helped that James had rushed off afterwards, claiming work was busy. She'd hoped they could talk.

Perhaps if they spent a morning together, her nerves would stop clanging. Pre-wedding nerves, right?

'You okay, hon?' Lisa asked as they left the church.

'Yes, Mom. I'm great.'

'Sure. Only, if you wanna talk, I'm here, okay?'

'There's nothing I need to talk about, but I appreciate the offer,' Goldie said, touched that her mother had noticed her nerves.

'You don't have to get married to this guy,' Lisa said.

'You came halfway across the world to see me get married. Wouldn't you be annoyed if I cancelled now?' Goldie teased weakly.

'I'd be full-on furious if you married the wrong guy. No pressure, kid. Do what's right for you.'

Lisa winked and then went to catch Dirk up. She slung her arm through his casually. Goldie thought that her mother had surely married the right guy. They were great together.

Lily appeared. She'd stopped to chat to the vicar. 'That went well, didn't it? I'm glad the last dress fittings are done too. I might scream if I have to get another pin stuck in me.'

'I'm glad it's over too. I'm going back to the hotel. Mom and Dad are going running, but I want to walk around and think about the reception. Are you coming?'

'I'll walk back with you, but I'm coming to get my mum. We're going over to my place to see the kittens. I can't wait to show her my garden; it's at its best just now. All the flowers are out. It's beautiful.'

Goldie smiled at Lily's enthusiasm. She might find the Smiths overpowering, but it was great that Lily was getting on well with them. She knew in the past that Lily hadn't had that closeness.

It was while wandering around the hotel gardens on her own that the feeling began to grow. It began as a prickling sensation on the back of her neck. Before long, it grew into a flush of heat and itchy bumps on her skin.

I'm breaking out in hives, Goldie thought, staring at the red lumps on the back of her hands. She felt them on her neck and face too. *I can't have hives when I'm getting married.*

She slumped onto a nearby wooden bench. It was cleverly placed to give a fine view of the herbaceous borders with their corncockles, marigolds and snapdragons swaying in the breeze.

'I'm getting hives *because* I'm getting married,' Goldie said out loud.

She gave a low moan. She'd wanted a Goldilocks wedding. The most perfect wedding imaginable. But it could never be that, because she was marrying the wrong man.

She clasped her hand over her mouth. Had she really let that thought escape? The trouble was, it was the truth. It had been creeping up on her. She didn't love James. She liked him very, very much. She loved his background and his lifestyle. But that wasn't enough to base a lifetime together on.

I can't cancel my wedding now, she thought. *It's too late. The church is booked, presents have arrived, and the reception and meal are paid for. Margery and Hugh must have all the ingredients in already. April's made my cake. Rose will expect to be paid for a photography job. Lily's so excited about her bridesmaid's dress. Oh, and we had the hen party. Dear goodness, what am I to do?*

She scratched at the hives in agitation. No solution presented itself. Her mind was a blank swirl of panic. She'd call Bryce. She always called Bryce if she had a problem or a quandary. She pulled her phone from her pocket. No, she couldn't. This was one problem she had to find an answer to herself. Bryce was the last person she could talk to about her wedding. They hadn't spoken since the night of the hen party. He was avoiding her. Goldie didn't want to see him, either. What would she say?

While she stared at her phone, it began to ring. Startled, she pressed the answer button. 'Hello?'

'It's me, James. Listen, Goldie, can you meet me at my office? I have to talk to you.

13

The car sales showroom was quiet. Goldie saw one salesman with a customer but that was all. Perhaps everyone was at the beach instead. Stella was missing, too. Goldie knocked on James's office door and went in without waiting.

James leapt up to greet her.

'Are you all right?' Goldie asked, 'Has something happened?'

'In a way,' James replied cryptically. 'We need to talk. I've sent Stella away on an errand so we can do so in peace without interruption.'

'Sounds serious,' she said lightly.

'Have you come out in a rash?' James said, frowning at her.

'It's a heat rash, nothing to worry about. So, what do we need to talk about?'

James pulled up two chairs. He sat in

one and nodded to the other. Goldie sat.

'I am really and truly sorry,' James said quietly, 'but I can't go through with our wedding.'

She should've felt stunned or horrified or sick to the stomach. If she was truly in love with James, any one of those reactions would have been normal. Instead, Goldie felt as if she was lifting up in a hot air balloon, getting lighter every minute that passed.

'Why not?' she said. She wanted to hear him out before she confessed to her own emotions.

'Because although I love you very much, I've realised that I'm not *in* love with you. Apparently there's a difference, only it's taken me far too long to work that out. I don't want to hurt you, but I can't marry you.'

'When did you discover the difference?'

'It was something that Stella said. You remember that evening I came for dinner and you asked me why I was 'antsy', as you put it?'

'Yes, I remember.' She'd thought he and Stella were having an affair. It sounded foolish now.

'I was telling her about the drop in car sales and she reassured me that it would recover. She said that time has a way of healing, and when you and I were old we'd look back on our life together and wonder why we worried so much.'

Goldie waited.

'Only, I couldn't imagine my whole life spent with you. It's awful, but I don't believe I'm cut out for marriage with anyone. I'm actually rather happy living on my own and focusing on my work.'

He looked so terribly upset that Goldie put her hand comfortingly on his. 'I'm so glad you've had the courage to tell me that,' she said, 'because I don't want to marry you, either. I'm extremely fond of you but I'm not in love with you. But the church is booked, the reception's organised, the guests are arriving and everyone is expecting a big wedding tomorrow. What on earth can we do?'

'You don't want to marry me?' James repeated.

'I'm sorry, but no.' Goldie smiled. 'I've been following a dream rather than a reality. I was so obsessed with my dream wedding that I forgot the mundane fact that we'd be stuck with each other forever afterwards. We're not made for each other, as it turns out, are we?'

James shook his head, but he was now smiling too. 'Can we be friends?'

Goldie thought of Bryce. Were they friends? She didn't know anymore.

'Yes, I'd like to stay friends,' she said. 'Any ideas how we cancel our wedding?'

James got up and paced about the large room. He steepled his fingers under his chin. Goldie watched. It took a good five minutes before he stopped in front of her. Goldie's own head was completely empty of ideas. All she could see were disappointed parents, a miserable Lily with a worthless bridesmaid's dress, and an angry April throwing cake at her.

'As you've said, we've already paid for the reception at the hotel, and the guests will have booked rooms and so forth. The meal is prepared, and I know all the food is in storage. The vicar has put us through our paces.'

'This isn't helping,' Goldie groaned. 'Now I feel worse than ever. We're letting everyone down.'

'Not if we have a party anyway. Obviously we let all our guests know we've called it off, and those who want to stay away can cancel their hotel bookings or guest-house rooms and so on. However, those who'd like to can join us for a summer party. I don't mind paying the costs. I'll never have a wedding, so I may as well enjoy this one.'

'James, that's quite marvellous. Off the wall, mad but marvellous,' Goldie said, with admiration. 'You're usually so traditional.'

James blushed. 'Not always, darling. Not always.'

* * *

'Tell me again. You and James are not getting married?' Lily said slowly, as if she didn't understand English. 'How can you not be getting married? The wedding's tomorrow.'

Goldie had gathered her friends for an emergency early evening coffee at their favourite cafe. Her announcement had met a stunned silence before Lily broke it. Rose looked upset for her, while April was sneaking a glance at her watch.

'James and I called it off.' Goldie gave them a summarised version of events. 'I wanted you guys to hear it from me face to face rather than the phone calls everyone else is getting. Although it looks like you've got something else on your mind, April?'

April jumped guiltily. 'Sorry, I'm going out to dinner tonight but I can spare an hour here.'

'Who're you going out to dinner with?' Rose asked with a sly smile. 'Let me guess.'

'Yes, it's Steve. He's my next-door neighbour,' April said to the others. 'It's only dinner.'

'He's taking you out on a date, isn't he?' Rose said.

Goldie and Lily stared at April, Goldie's big news momentarily put to one side. April had a date? This was massive.

'He's taking me out on a date,' April said and a slow, dopey smile widened her mouth.

They all clapped until she scowled and told them to stop.

'Anyway, back to Goldie,' Lily said. 'What are you going to do?'

'We're both happy with our decision, so no one needs to feel sorry for us. We've decided to have a summer party tomorrow instead. Will you all come?'

Rose gave a small cough. They looked at her.

'I don't know if this is the right time or not. But I have some news too. Only I don't want to upset you, Goldie.'

'I promise I won't be upset. I feel liberated and not at all sad.'

'Well, Ben and I are engaged.'

There were whoops of joy from Rose's three best friends, and Goldie called for some champagne, only to be told they didn't stock it. Soon, four glasses of sparkling wine joined the coffee cups and cake crumbs on the table.

'I have a great idea,' Goldie said once they'd drunk a toast to Rose and Ben's future. 'Why don't we celebrate with an engagement party tomorrow?'

'We couldn't possibly,' Rose protested. 'You've paid for it all.'

'Nonsense,' Goldie brushed her argument aside. 'James paid for most of it, and he doesn't care to see the money back. We're having the party in any case, so why not make it special and launch your engagement? Please say you will.'

'If you want to,' Rose said. 'If you're sure.'

It was all settled. All that remained was to tell James's parents and her own. Somehow, Goldie didn't think her mom and dad would be at all surprised. As for the Smiths, they might be relieved to find James wasn't going to be marrying beneath him after all.

★   ★   ★

The big day dawned bright and clear. Goldie smiled wryly as she stared out of the window. She couldn't have picked a better date to get married on. It was every bride's dream to be wed under warm sunshine, and so perfect for the wedding photographs too.

She felt as though she'd done a fantastic workout as she stretched her body and grabbed a towel for her shower. She was full of energy, full of happiness and best of all, her hives had completely disappeared. She wasn't marrying James and it was okay. Better than okay. They were to remain friends, and that was what mattered most of all.

Once dressed in a light turquoise silk skirt and white blouse, she brushed her long blonde curls, applied some makeup and decided it was time to head to the Mansion House Hotel to help prepare for the afternoon party.

It should have been awkward meeting with Margery and Hugh to make the final decisions on how the catering was to be laid out and who was sitting where, but somehow it wasn't. Goldie got the distinct impression that they were relieved their only son was not to marry this American outsider. Of course, they were too polite to say so.

In fact, they were warmer to Goldie than they had ever been. She reckoned staying friends with James would be even easier now that she had discovered some rapport with his parents.

Margery took her to one side while the men arrived to put up the marquee on the lawn. 'I wanted to say how sorry I am that it didn't work out with James. Are you all right?'

Goldie was suddenly touched by how kind James's mother was. They were very different, and she found Margery quite old-fashioned, but now she began to see that underneath her rather stuffy exterior was a gentle and thoughtful woman.

'I am all right, thank you,' Goldie said. 'James and I have been lucky enough to discover we're better as friends than husband and wife before we married. I'm sure some couples may only realise this after the knot is tied.'

Margery reached out and patted her hand. 'You would have made me a very lovely daughter-in-law, but I hope we can be friends too.'

'I'd like that.'

'Now, back to practicalities,' Margery said, shoulders back and face serious. 'The marquee is up and we'll put in tables and chairs. Do you want the champagne served as the guests file into their seats? We've had a few weddings where that happens, and it goes down well.'

'Sounds great.' Goldie hesitated. 'Margery . . . does this all seem odd to you? That instead of a wedding reception for your son, you're organising an engagement party for two people you don't know?'

Margery laughed. It was a horsey, wheezing noise that was infectious, and soon Goldie was laughing too. Their giggles went on for some while before they both stopped and gasped.

'Oh dear, I needed that.' Margery blew her nose into a large white handkerchief. 'Odd doesn't really cover it, does it? Anyway, you mustn't worry. James did sit us down and explain that he wanted to spend the money on this. He was quite adamant. Who am I to argue with my only son?'

Goldie wiped her streaming eyes. It was nice to be crying tears of laughter instead of sadness for a change. 'As long as you're okay with it. I'm so happy for Rose and Ben, and they can't afford a big engagement party like this, so I'm pleased they'll get one.'

'Are all the original wedding guests invited?'

'Yes, and most are coming simply for a chance to get together, even if they don't know Rose or Ben. Some have cancelled their bookings, as you know, but they were relatives coming from far afield so I quite understand. Obviously there are Rose and Ben's friends and family now too.'

The guest list included Bryce. Goldie hadn't had the nerve to tell him herself. She'd phoned Morag instead. Morag had said how sorry she was that it hadn't worked out and that she would love to come to the engagement party and she'd let Bryce know. Goldie didn't know if he'd turn up. She didn't know if she wanted him to.

The next few hours passed quickly as she helped organise for the party. James turned up and kissed her chastely on the cheek. They had made the change from engaged couple to old friends without a phase in between, but it worked.

The party was due to begin at midday with champagne and canapés. Then there was to be music on the lawn and a buffet lunch with dancing later.

Goldie's parents were the first to arrive. They thrived on punctuality, so she wasn't surprised to see them. She *was* surprised when they both embraced her. Dirk landed a firm kiss on her head while Lisa hugged her hard.

'How are you, honey?'

'I'm fine. How are you? Are you mad that the wedding's off? You came all the way to England for nothing.'

'Not for nothing. We came to see our little girl. We don't see enough of you, we're so hectic, but maybe you'll come visit us soon?'

Goldie hugged them back, her heart fit to burst. She loved them so much. It turned out they loved her too. She'd known that deep down, of course, but it was nice when they showed it.

'I'll come and visit you. I'd love to see the States again.'

'It's a date. We'll set up it as soon as we get back Stateside. Now we're holding up the queue, so we'd better get along to the marquee, hon.'

Rose and Ben were next to arrive. Rose was glowing, her cheeks pink with joy, complementing her cherry-red dress nicely. Ben had a protective arm around her and a wide smile that wouldn't go away.

'The happy couple,' Goldie cried, kissing them both. 'Come along in; this is your party.'

'Are you truly okay with this?' Rose asked. 'It should've been your party.'

'I feel fantastic,' Goldie said truthfully. 'Please enjoy the afternoon.'

Ben pulled his fiancée in a little closer, and Rose gazed up at him in delight. Goldie realised the two were very much in love. She'd never looked at James like that, nor he at her.

'Thanks for this,' Ben said to her.

'We'll never forget this day. Tomorrow we're going to pick out engagement rings.'

She let them through and watched them go to the marquee and chat with Lisa and Dirk. There was a definite aura around them. The lawn began to fill with the other guests, and soon the sound of laughter and chat filled the air. Waitresses offered drinks and canapés, and people stood in little groups or sat at the tables. The band played soft music in the background.

Goldie breathed in the sweet air. It was all so perfect. She saw April and Steve talking with Rose and Ben. April looked relaxed and younger. Instead of her usual smart but severe suits, she was wearing a pretty flower-patterned dress belted at the waist and low-heeled sandals. She was managing without her crutches by using Steve's arm for support. Her hair was softly waved and had grown over the summer so that it framed her face and accentuated her blue eyes. She looked lovely, Goldie thought fondly. Steve was good for her. Perhaps there'd be another engagement party in the not-too-distant future.

The chat and music were suddenly cut by the loud sound of an engine backfiring. An ancient campervan swung to a halt on the edge of the car park amid a puff of black smoke. Lily descended from it with a wide grin. She was wearing her bridesmaid dress, a wonderful creation of green silk with a nipped-in waist and flaring skirts. She looked dramatic and wonderful.

'Hello,' she called, waving to Goldie. 'How's the party going? Sorry I'm late, but the van wouldn't start.'

April and Rose came over too, and the four friends greeted each other, exclaiming over Lily's beautiful dress.

'I didn't want to waste it,' Lily explained with a grin. 'After all, I spend many long hours being pricked by pins to get it made. You don't mind, do you?' She looked at Goldie and the grin slipped. 'I never thought . . . I'm such an idiot . . . this reminds you of your wedding.'

Goldie shook her head and smiled. 'I love that you've worn it. It's a gorgeous dress and it's perfect for celebrating Rose's engagement. At least it'll get some wear, unlike my dress, which is hanging up on the wardrobe door in its plastic wrap. I'll probably sell it.'

'You might get to wear it yet,' April said with a sly nudge and a meaningful look over Goldie's shoulder.

Puzzled, Goldie turned to see where April was staring. Her skin prickled as if the temperature had rapidly changed. Her heartbeat was uneven and she had to swallow. Bryce was walking towards them. Behind him, she saw Morag wave and then head into the marquee.

She turned to say something offhand to her friends, only to find they had melted away into the crowd. She stood there, clutching the stem of her empty glass, words vanished and mouth dry.

Bryce smiled as he stood before her. He was taller than usual, Goldie thought hazily. Or was that because he was standing closer to her than normal? She had to crane her neck to look him in the eye. And that was a mistake, because once their gazes met, she couldn't look away.

'You're not getting married?' Bryce murmured, his eyes never leaving hers.

'Seems not.' There was a catch in her voice.

Immediately, his expression changed to concern. 'You're upset. You wanted to get married. James ditched you? Why, I'll — '

'No, no.' She shook her head emphatically. 'We both called it off. It was mutual.'

Bryce's shoulders relaxed, and a slow smile returned to lighten his features. He moved in closer, and she felt his breath ruffle her hair and smelt his fragrance. Something spicy but familiar, too. She knew him so well.

'Bryce . . . about the night of the hen party . . . what you said . . . '

'I was a fool,' he murmured.

'So we can be friends now?' There

was no reason not to be, she thought. She wasn't getting married, so she and Bryce could go back to the way things had been.

'I don't want to be friends.'

Goldie's heart plummeted. It was painful. She dropped the glass and didn't notice when it miraculously bounced in the grass and didn't break. Bryce didn't want to be friends. He didn't like her anymore. She'd lost him.

'I don't want to be friends, my darling,' Bryce said. 'I want to be your husband.'

Without waiting for an answer, he leaned down and kissed her thoroughly. Goldie clung to him and kissed him back just as fervently. She wanted to marry Bryce. She was going to tell him so. Then she was going to start planning her dream wedding, her Goldilocks wedding with him. But that could all wait. Right now, all she wanted to do was to kiss him until she saw the stars.

We do hope that you have enjoyed reading this large print book.

Did you know that all of our titles are available for purchase?

We publish a wide range of high quality large print books including:
Romances, Mysteries, Classics
General Fiction
Non Fiction and Westerns

Special interest titles available in large print are:
The Little Oxford Dictionary
Music Book, Song Book
Hymn Book, Service Book

Also available from us courtesy of Oxford University Press:
Young Readers' Dictionary
(large print edition)
Young Readers' Thesaurus
(large print edition)

For further information or a free brochure, please contact us at:
Ulverscroft Large Print Books Ltd.,
The Green, Bradgate Road, Anstey,
Leicester, LE7 7FU, England.
Tel: (00 44) **0116 236 4325**
Fax: (00 44) **0116 234 0205**